-+>==◉ ◉==+<-

Advance praise for *The Agriculture Hall of Fame*

"The Kansas of *The Agriculture Hall of Fame* is brokedown, hardluck country. Andrew Malan Milward's precarious, paralyzed people are lost in place, and know it, alternately circling and fleeing the center of the center of America. As one says, 'Out here, everybody's crazy with looking for something.' Wry and sad, this is a fine debut collection."

—STEWART O'NAN, author of *The Odds*

"Andrew Malan Milward is a subtle writer with an unsparing eye and a heart as vast as a prairie. The ten stories in his first book, *The Agriculture Hall of Fame*, are graceful evocations of loss—of fathers and first loves, of lakes and sisters, of the rusting midwestern heartland one sees from a bus window as it pulls away. An evocative debut from a writer to cheer for."

—LAUREN GROFF, author of *Delicate Edible Birds:*
And Other Stories and *Arcadia*

The Agriculture Hall of Fame

The Agriculture Hall of Fame

⊷⊶ STORIES ⊷⊶

Andrew Malan Milward

University of Massachusetts Press
Amherst & Boston

Designed by Jack Harrison
Set in Quadraat with Monotype Bernard Condensed display
Printed and bound by The Maple-Vail Book Manufacturing Group

Library of Congress Cataloging-in-Publication Data
Milward, Andrew Malan.
The agriculture hall of fame : stories / Andrew Malan Milward.
p. cm.
ISBN 978-1-55849-948-5 (pbk. : alk. paper)
I. Title.
PS3613.I59I99A73 2012
813'.6—dc23
2012003646

British Library Cataloguing in Publication data are available.

For two Janes, Stoneback and Milward.
Heroes both.

I navigate us across Kansas and into a large ruined area
where crumpled fenders and auto parts are lying about.
It is hard to find an exit.

ANNE CARSON, "The Anthropology of Water"

It takes a worried man to sing a worried song.

"Worried Man Blues," traditional

Contents

The Agriculture Hall of Fame

Quail Haven, 1989

OUR FATHER COMES HOME from work, grumbling and flatulent. He steps out of the old Ford and into the house and grunts, brushing past my brother and me as we try to grab hold of his belt loops and pull at the cuffs of his trousers. We follow him around, picking up his tie, abruptly loosed at five o'clock, and gently we lay it at the foot of the bed. And then our mother appears, smoothing the lines of her apron, unaware of that spot of flour that has collected on her cheek, spat from a thunderous rolling pin. She follows a step and half behind him, asking questions, as he paces around the room. Our father pushes her out of the way and sits on the corner of the bed, slouch-backed, because he's been "answering questions all day and needs to fucking decompress." He takes off his black nylon socks, balls them up, and throws one at us—"Here, catch, you little monsters"—while the other hits the rim of the hamper and falls to floor, swallowed up by some dark corner of the bedroom. When no one's looking we can't help but raise the damp sock to our noses and inhale.

At dinner he jabs at the food on his plate and then stands, grabs a dripping Miller from the fridge, and moves to the window. He looks out at the sky that illuminates the land, his land, all these acres that had been his father's and grandfather's before him. "Going out to the barn," he might say, though sometimes he just breaks wind and leaves. Our mother's mouth opens, as though she might rejoinder, and then she looks to us, hoping for answers. "Why do you never speak?" My brother looks at me, then we at her, silent. We tine through our food while in our minds we follow our stumbling father out to the barn, and in doing so we begin to understand him.

The barn is where he keeps his secrets, the echoes of long ago that toll endlessly still, the unspeakable and sad: the greening class ring and broken-armed trophies; the lacy underwear of girlfriends gone by that on occasion, when the loneliness is overwhelming, he wraps around his index finger and brushes against his cheek, remembering; the letters his buddies gave him during the war to give to their families just in case—those epistles he could never bring himself to deliver when he returned home from that other world, still reading over his friends' words, so familiar now, mouthing along. Our father is a stark mosaic of his past: his maimed seven-year-old feet, dappled by a friend's errant buckshot; the 8-to-5 creases framing his adulterous eyes; the broken-down All-State throwing arm, forever aching; his red, swollen knuckles and Vietnam brain.

We watch the lights of Quail Haven (or others of the like—there are hundreds of them across the Kansas plains falling apart or being torn down, disappearing) turn on from the window above the sink. Our mother scrapes plates and then goes to stand before the washer and dryer, mesmerized by the synergistic pulse. She silently curses the day the state decided not to build a highway through this stretch of land. She holds out a dim hope, like a smoldering ember, that someday she will be allowed to sell this place and move to Kansas City like so many old friends, because "Who the hell lives in the country anymore?"

Of course, we're not totally imagining him, our father. We know a little. There was that night when, after a small promotion at the office and several slugs of bourbon, he brought us out there with him. And as we reached the entrance of the barn he stopped and held us up to pull the lever that would give us light to see in the dark. Against his chest we could smell the heat on his breath, causing our eyes to water, and then the lights turned on one by one, illuminating a single section of Quail Haven at a time. And at this threshold, our father was unable to say anything—no stories about how our great-granddad built Quail Haven all those years ago, or how he lost his virginity right over there in the hardwood loft, or the boxing matches he used to have here with his brother (the one who died in the war, whom we know only through a single picture, warped as parchment) while their father looked on, grinning, leaning against the splintery siding, thumbs snaked through denim belt loops.

This is where our mother will find him a decade later, on the cusp of the millennium, hanging from a cross beam, slowly turning in the still air, and feel the immense burden fly from her shoulders. But that night, the night he brought us out there with him, was different. When the last light came on inside Quail Haven, the vast silence of it all shot fear through my brother and me, like the time we entered an empty church before our first funeral, causing us to grip him harder, tighter. We stood there, the three of us, unmoving. And that silence seemed to offer two possibilities: one that would finally let us speak, and the other, like a gaping mouth, that would swallow us whole.

Skywriting

CHICKEN AND VALIUM

"HOUSES THIS BIG should be called estates," said M as she got out of the car, pulling her long, black dreads off her shoulders and into a ponytail. We stood in the driveway, taking in the place I was to watch while my mother's friends were out of town for the Fourth of July weekend. I knew the Mission Hills homes were big, but living in a hole on 39th St. hadn't provided many encounters with the Kansas City elite, these people who won awards for their mailboxes. At twenty-seven I felt ashamed for taking such a handout from my mom but was desperate enough to accept; I'd recently lost my job as a bar-back at lawyer bar downtown and the first of the month was near.

In the waxing shadow of the mansion, I looked around at the almost surgical precision of the grounds, someone's topiary dream world. This house was less than a mile away from the modest three-bedroom where I'd grown up, from where my mom still lived—over on the Missouri side of State Line Road in an area called Brookside—but it might as well have been another world. I counted the windows stretching across the second story, eighteen of them. It made me feel like I often had working at the bar: all those drunken lawyers with their fierce, ruddy faces and thousand-dollar suits, gulping down premium vodkas and yelling at me to clear their table or to bring them another drink—that feeling of knowing that these goddamn people had more money than I could ever hope to comprehend.

We entered the house through the garage using the code my mom had given me over the phone. I hadn't seen her since I started up with M and we hadn't spoken in a few weeks, since I'd called her asking for a loan again. "I'm keeping tabs on all this," I'd said. "I'll pay you back once a job comes through." She didn't say anything and the silence hung between us like a burdened clothesline. In the ten years since my dad died my mom and I had been moving in opposite directions, her towards the church and me further away from not only it, but college, steady work, a settled life. Finally, she said she couldn't give me the loan. "Can't," I said, "or won't?" I'd been in and out of substance-support groups for several years and I knew she suspected the money was for drugs. She said she'd help me out if I enrolled at the community college, if I made positive steps in my life. I could start by coming to church with her that weekend, she said, and I was hanging up the phone before the words "Never mind" were out of my mouth.

I will admit I believe she really did love me and wanted only for me to be better. The problem was that I did too and that hadn't seemed to change much for me.

A few days later, my mom called back and told me about this house-sitting gig. She said it was out of the kindness of the hearts of her friends from church. "I hope this helps you find your way out of the desert, Steven," she said, and when I didn't respond she added: "You'll blink and you'll be thirty and still trying to find your way out."

M and I opened the door to find a bulldog looking up at us from the kitchen floor. I thought it might jump up and take my leg in its mouth like a drumstick, but it just sat there, chin on the tile floor, like, *What do you want from me?* We moved inside cautiously. There was the lemony smell of dusted shelves and clean countertops. Large bay windows looked out on a garden that could have charged an admission fee. I could make out a swarm of mutant bumblebees, junkied for pollen. There was a note on the island written in small cursive script on stationery headed *Mrs. John Sherman.*

"Your mom's friends with these people?" said M.

"Yeah, sort of."

"She loaded like this?"

"Not hardly," I said. "They just go to the same church, this huge one out in Olathe." They were Born Agains. The Shermans must have pitied my mom, widowed and mother to a prodigal son whose name had been read aloud from the prayer list every Sunday for the last ten years. I said, "My mom's nothing like these people," but all I meant was her bank account was nothing like theirs.

Mrs. Sherman's note said I didn't need to worry about the garden; there was a "team" to handle that. I was, however, to feed the dog, Sally, an entire can of chicken twice a day along with a tablet of Valium, once in the morning and once at night. I could almost hear the voice that had written: *She has been depressed lately. I apologize in advance for any tempestuousness. She can be a real devil—the Valium should help.* Behind me M opened the fridge, which I'd later find populated by an array of premium condiments: mustards, capers, olives, and pimentos. I looked down at Sally with her drooping, rheumy eyes and then at the little amber bottle next to the note. It was almost full. My mind fluttered with possibility. Underneath the bottle was a check for two hundred dollars.

At the very bottom of the note, as the weight from her hand's impress had eased, there was a final underlined imperative: *Absolutely no guests in the house!* I could hear M breathing as she looked out the window at the garden.

"What's she say?"

"Not much," I answered. "The dog's on Valium."

EL DORADO

M's lunch break was almost over, so I dropped her back at the record store to finish her shift and went to the bank. I would make a deposit, pay rent, and be clear for another month while I tried to find a job. This was my mantra as I walked toward the building, and this is what I tried to forget five minutes later as I walked back to my car with all but $50 in cash. There was a not-too-distant time when I would have used it all to score on the Paseo. Now, however, I was a man of good intentions and, while that was about it, I liked the idea of having money in my pocket, of being, however little, a man of means.

This whole thing with M was still new. We'd only been together for about a month, and our bodies were still learning how to occupy the same space. So there was that. But there was this other thing, too: two years before, when she was twenty-three, she'd been busted selling thirty hits of blotter acid to an undercover cop at a head shop. By the time we met at the NA meeting her P.O. required her to attend, she'd come out of the halfway house only weeks before. Needless to say, things still felt strange to her. In the space of five minutes she could go from furious, to sad, to completely loving. There were times when I'd hold her and I could tell she *needed* me, and that felt good, as if by helping her I might find my own way.

Me? That story begins with light drugs as early as fourteen, before my dad died, and only later did I fall deep into meth, and that was some kind of hole to find myself in. I'd resisted interventions from my mom and members of her church and started going to groups on my own. The day M showed up I knew she was a girl I had to meet. The first thing she ever said to me was, "My name is Maeve, but if you ever call me that I'll punch your eye out." We would talk in the parking lot after meetings as the others smoked and soon she was telling me to come visit her at the record store. On her lunch breaks we'd walk to a nearby lake and swim. She always wore a swimsuit under her clothes so she could go swimming at a moment's notice. God, she loved the water. I didn't, but I would go with her and sit on the bank, shirtless with a beer in hand, as she swam. There, treading water in the lake, she'd tell me about what it was like inside.

She once told me that in County she'd fallen in love with an inmate from Peru, a guy named Hector. "The crazy thing about Hector was we never spoke," she said on one of those afternoons at the lake. "We communicated though." She raised her hand from the water, letting it run off her fingers. The glint of the sun on the water made me squint. "This thing, we called it skywriting. A lot of us did it." She explained that since men and women were on separate sides of the jail, they would look at each other through the steel-barred windows and use their hands to write to one another, spelling out individual letters in the air each night until the light failed. She lost herself in those conversations. It made time pass and that, I imagine, is all anyone inside ever wants. Which is why it was so devastating when she came up for sentencing and the judge shipped her off to prison in El Dorado, Kansas. "Going there meant leaving Hector, our conversations," she said, tilting her face up to the afternoon sun. "That's when we started writing fifty-page letters, telling each other every thought that passed through our heads." I remember the white of her cheeks were starting to burn. "Know something?" she continued. "We made plans, me and Hector." *Plans?* I wondered, sipping my beer. "When our parole is up. I'm moving down there."

"Peru?" I laughed.

Her hand flew out of the water like a jumping fish and slapped my leg red. "Yeah, Peru, asshole," she said. "You don't believe me, do you? We're gonna have a family and grow our own food. Hector will fish and I'll start an organic farm. I'm gonna have like a dozen of his babies."

And me, I wanted to ask, would I make the thatch hunt and tan leather for our sandals?

Her face was earnest and angry. "You can be a real asshole sometimes," she said. I concurred, and she dunked herself under water, staying down thirty seconds or so, and when she came up she was smoothing the water back through her dreads, smiling again.

You Are Trying to Kill Me

In group, they called trading one addiction for another "substitution" and while I'd been off meth for over a year I hadn't given up drinking. I used some of the house-sitting money to buy beer and went back to the Shermans'. I let Sally out and fixed her chicken and Valium. I was sipping on a longneck and held the bottle of Valium in my hand. I fastened the cap and set it on the island. I picked it back up and set it down again. I did this a few more times before taking a long pull of beer and walking away. I decided to explore, going from room to room, looking at their closets and furniture, wondering if they'd notice a missing item. I touched everything and took nothing.

On the way to pick up M, I stopped to get a pizza for dinner. The smell filled the car, so that when M opened the door she said, "God, it's like a fucking cheese sauna in here." I'd made a mistake though and when M flipped open the box back at the Shermans' she said, "What the hell is this?"

We were standing at the island in the kitchen.

"It's a veggie," I said.

"I see that," she said, "and I'm vegan. This has cheese on both halves."

Sometimes I forgot.

"You can't eat cheese?" I grinned, hoping cajolery might make her forsake ethics.

"No meat, no cheese," she said, walking to the cupboards. "Thanks for ruining dinner."

"You're impossible." Sometimes she made me want to strut around in leather fucking chaps with a turkey leg in each hand, Henry VIII style.

"There's nothing to eat it this house," she said, slamming the cupboard door. "These people are rich—where the hell's all their food?"

"Calm down."

"You're not the boss of me."

I loved how she said things like this with complete sincerity. It always made me laugh.

"Fuck you for laughing at me," she said. She flipped the lid of the pizza box again. "I don't know how you put that in your body."

I beat my fingers against my chest and said, "This heart is made of red meat."

"You're filthy! You're unclean," she said. "I'm being serious. Listen to me." She took a moment to compose herself. "There are other ways to live that are healthier and don't involve killing living things."

"Vegetables are living things," I said. "Plants, too."

"Don't be a dick." We were both quiet and Sally looked up at me, her drooling so expectant. Again M opened the pizza box and considered it.

"Can you pick off the cheese?" I said.

She nudged the crust with her finger and looked up suddenly. "You are trying to kill me."

That night M sulked so long that I gave her money to go to the store to buy food. I gave her more than she needed and she snatched the money from my hand and took my car keys from the table. I waited until she was out of hearing distance and then called out "Please come back" into the empty house, after which I set ardently to figuring out how to work the television. She returned sometime later with an armful of organic booty: a can of garbanzo beans, a box of whole-wheat pasta, tofu, and oblong vegetables I had no name for. I waited to eat the pizza until she came back and it was dead cold. I was kneeling in front of the monstrous television pressing buttons and she took a seat on the couch, tucking her feet underneath her, grinning as she watched me fuss around with technology.

"Where's my change?" I said.

"I used it all."

"Are you lying?"

"You're accusing me of thievery," she said.

"Thievery? What are we in the middle ages? I just thought maybe there was some change."

"Well there isn't."

"Ugh," I said.

"Ugh," she replied.

Finally, some combination of buttons worked and the picture came on. Instinctively, I threw my hands up, the caveman sparking fire. We flipped through five hundred channels, not stopping long enough on any to get the full story. We drank and spent some time on the softcore channels, critiquing the finer points of simulated sex. "Would you look at her face," M said. "He doesn't even have it inside her. What a faker."

"It's the idea though," I defended my brother on screen. "She thinks she'd have a nice time with him."

Mrs. Sherman's note had said to stay in one of the guestrooms she called "the blue room." The dulling buzz of a whole night of drinking made my hands feel like paddles as I led M upstairs. It seemed like it might be an endeavor to find this blue room.

We collapsed into bed, a tangle of limbs, and taking off our clothes might have been the most burdensome chore that day. It was dark in the room, the blue walls covered in night. The guestroom, one of three I counted that day as I wandered through the place, seemed like it hadn't been used in years. M lay on my chest and it felt like she might sink into me and I'd lose myself forever. I kissed the top of her wooly head and she looked up at me. I said hello.

"Hey," she said, and her eyes closed.

It was weird. I was asleep and then we were having sex. Apparently I'd joined events already in progress, as though my dream self couldn't wait any longer for me to get my act together with such a beautiful woman lying next to me. There was a moment where I thought, *Shit, the condom*, but if I were an honest man I'd also say that in that instant I didn't care, and then I was back with M, unthinking, lost somewhere in the circuit our bodies had made.

I woke early and left M to sleep a little longer. Downstairs, I let Sally out and fed her. I wandered around in my boxers, giving my balls a good morning scratch, and opened a door I assumed was a pantry only to find a stairway that led to a basement. I'd missed this when I was exploring. Amazing, that secret room. Bunkerlike, it was unfinished and there were floor-to-ceiling shelves crammed full of canned goods and boxed foods. There must have been a dozen mousetraps scattered like a minefield across the cold cement floor. I tiptoed around the room. There were two more fridges, stainless steel, big as you'd expect to find in the kitchen of a restaurant. They were packed with food and drink. I'd heard stories about how Mormon families stockpile goods they'll need when the End comes. The Shermans were preparing for Rapture. I scanned the labels in the fridge and picked up some bottled water and a carton of ice cream from the freezer.

I wanted to tell M about the basement, but she wasn't in bed. I couldn't find her anywhere in fact. I called out her name and stormed up and down the hallways, popping in and out of every room. In one of the bathrooms I heard a strange sound. Someone breathing heavily. I stood before the sink and caught a glimpse of something moving in the mirror. I turned around and looked in the tub. There she was, lying flat in a waterless bath, arms crossed over her chest. Her eyes were wild and looked right through me. I asked her what was wrong.

She said, "Where were you?"

MATH

County: 7 months
Prison: 5 months
Halfway: 1 year
Out: 2 months
I tried to remember these facts.

THE WATER

We sat at the kitchen table, silent. What does one say to someone who's had two years of her life stolen? I put my hand on her leg and rubbed softly. Maybe it was only to make me stop, but she took my hand in hers and we sat there looking out the window at the next-door neighbor. He was cleaning the grill and setting up croquet stakes and a badminton net. I'd forgotten it was the Fourth of July.

I told her about the basement and the food, but she didn't seem to carry my bewilderment. "Kinda weird," she said. I asked if I could get her some breakfast and she said I could bring her a beer. We drank for some time and soon M seemed to feel better. When she drained her third, she said, "This is how everyone should wake up on national holidays."

"I'm feeling famished," I said, though I'd never used that word before, rubbing my hands over my stomach. I went to the freezer for ice cream and opened the lid, jamming in the only spoon I could find. It was about the size one would use to feed a baby its goop. "What is it with these people?" I said, holding it up for M to see. The ice cream had thawed and frozen again, so it was stubbly with frost. I held the carton to my chest like a newborn and paced around the island, flinging the freezer burnt chunks at Sally, who trailed behind me. I felt nervous all of a sudden. I was thinking about sex and I was thinking about condoms, which is exactly what I announced to M.

"Enlighten me on these subjects," she said.

"Well, I'm thinking we're not suitable parents and that we should go to a clinic." This was back when you couldn't get the morning-after pill over the counter.

"You pulled out though, right?"

"It's not an exact science," I said, ramming more ice cream into my mouth. I could feel it building, slow but unmistakable. I was in the first trimester of a torturous brain-freeze.

"I think we'll be okay," she said.

"Perhaps we'd benefit from a second opinion." If only I could stop eating the damn ice cream. My sponsor once said I had a tendency toward self-destruction when I called him at three in the morning for a week straight, saying I had a wad of bills in one hand and my car keys in the other. I leaned forward onto the island and raised my hands to my head.

"What's wrong with you?"

"Nothing," I said, making this weird face, like I was playing the greatest guitar solo ever.

Then the negotiations began. M was unforgiving at the bargaining table and later it was decided that she would go to the clinic, but only after I took her to the water. She didn't mean our usual lake though. She wanted to go to a lake clear out in the center of the state, a couple hundred miles. It was the largest freshwater lake in Kansas and she'd never been. "I hate swimming in all this man-made shit, you know."

I didn't know, and said, "Do you know how long that will take? No, we'll stop at the clinic on our way out of town and be done with it." I'd begun gesturing wildly with my hands and was getting into using them for accent. "I'm making the decisions here. I'm older—I have more authority!"

"You're not the boss of me!" she said. She should have had this tattooed on a butt cheek.

"I'm not about to become a father."

"It's okay," she said. "I can take the pill tomorrow, Steve. Two days is okay."

I didn't want to pursue this line of questioning any further, because all of a sudden the ghost of every man she'd ever slept with was in the room with us.

The Shermans wouldn't be back until Sunday night. Before we left, I let Sally out, put extra food in her bowl, and soon we were on the road. The Kansas highway stretched on endlessly. My poor little car, a Yugo my father purchased when it was sensible to do such things, was like a salmon battling upstream whenever I pushed seventy. The passing billboards said things like *Hell is REAL* and *1 Kansas Farmer Feeds 130 People + You*. We stopped at an exit where there was a Phillips 66 and a Fireworks Emporium. I filled up the tank and she went to use the bathroom. While M was still inside I went over to the fireworks shop, where they were having a Fourth of July sale. I picked up several bandoliers of Black Cats and some bottle rockets.

We drove on a while in silence until suddenly M shouted for me to pull over.

"What's wrong?"

"Just do it!" she screamed.

I thought *Morning sickness already? No way!* as I pulled over the rumble strips onto the gravelly shoulder. "Back up," she said. I put the car in reverse and drove back thirty yards or so, again asking what was wrong. She opened the door and yelled "Come on" over her shoulder as she ran out into the adjacent field. There were no clouds in the sky, just the unrelenting heat from the sun. I surveyed the horizon. Nothing, just miles of empty land. Then I realized why she wanted me to stop. There were orange zoning flags all over the place. The land was being developed, destined to become endless tracts of Stuckey's and Cabela's. M shouted: "This land used to be a farm, you know. It used to feed people!" She began pulling out the flags, running from one to the next, looking at me looking at her. "Come on," she said, pulling out another and throwing it. "It fucks them all up. They won't remember where they put them." I stood still; the developers would have plans and zoning maps. Of course they would remember. But there was something about watching her in that field that made me reach for that first one. She believed. M looked at me pulling out the flag and yelled, "Yeah, the bastards!" and threw one over her shoulder.

After we'd removed all the zoning flags and put them in a pile, M sat down next to me on the ground. The air was humid and my shirt was completely soaked through. We were both exhausted. "I love this sultry weather," she said, looking up at the sky, smiling.

"What are we going to do with all these flags?" I said.

"Throw them in your trunk. We'll get rid of them later."

The whole time I was sure a county sheriff or statey was going to drive by and arrest us, but nothing ever happened, except that for a brief moment I had believed, too. I sat there, trying to understand why she would risk breaking parole and being sent back to prison. How do we ever make sense of one another? She was a mystery, an enigma, part of some strange order of souls who love the earth but hate the world.

After an endless search for a place that met M's dietary needs, we ate lunch in a town we seemed to will into existence with our arrival. She ordered and went to sit down at a table, leaving me to pay. The fold of bills in my wallet was shrinking. I tried to tell myself it was a holiday and that I was celebrating with my girlfriend. And then I thought of rent. As we ate quietly, I remembered watching a movie where a guy falls asleep in a department store and is locked inside after it closes. He likes it so much that he does it for the next month until he's finally caught. In a moment of fiery genius I fantasized of breaking into Wal-Mart and hiding out in the auto-care area behind some tires, fancying I could make a pretty good go of it in there.

BOB

I'd learn his name was Bob, but when we arrived at the boat rental office he was just a man standing outside holding a green garden hose in a shirt that said *Jesus—don't leave home without Him.* M told him we needed a boat, so we followed him inside and looked at the price sheet. I told him I didn't know if I had enough money.

"Can you work with me, brother," I said.

"I like the look of you youngsters," he said, extending his hand. "Let's see what the Lord can help us do here." Surely if there weren't a counter between us I would have been nose deep in his shoulder, feeling the full weight of Christian love. Bob reminded me of my mom's friends. Warm and completely terrifying. When she started up at the church, it was after my dad died, and until I moved out a couple years later it seemed there was always one or two of them hanging around the house, talking sin and redemption. They made me nervous because they wanted so much from me. I had not accepted Jesus Christ as my personal savior.

Bob scratched his bald head with the sharp end of a pencil and punched some numbers into a computer, repeating, "Hold on now. Praise be, let's see here."

With what I was offering, which was all but gas money for the ride home, he said I could afford to take a boat out over night and return it in the morning. "The boat'll get you along the shores to some of the beaches. Otherwise, I could rent you a canoe for cheaper."

"These are my options," I said.

Bob gave me a quick lesson on how to operate the boat and soon we were in the water. He said it was extra busy because of the holiday. There were so many boats on the lake I was sure I'd crash right into one. I asked if there was anywhere that was quiet and he pointed in the distance towards what he called the best beach no one knew about. It took a little while, but we made our way out. Occasionally I looked over my shoulder at M, who was dragging her hand through the water and looking into the depths. When we arrived, I grabbed my bag of fireworks and followed her down the ladder to the shore.

It was a small beach and Bob was right. There was only one other group, three girls and two guys, who looked like they could still be in college. They were sitting in a circle with a 30-pack of Olympia between them, trying to shape the sand into a topless bust of a mermaid. I was expecting to tiptoe across the sand, but with the sun now obscured it was cool, cold even. We walked to the other end of the beach. We had no towels so we just sat there and looked out at the massive lake.

"Gonna blow something up?" she asked, jutting her chin at the fireworks.

"Don't know. Maybe," I said. "How's the water look?"

"Looks alright," she said. After a minute of silence she added, "The only thing my family ever did together was go to the beach. Twice a year we'd visit family in Cape May and spend every second at the shore. My parents would fight the entire time, but I didn't care."

"Sounds like my folks," I said. I thought of all those nights where from the cover of bed or a cracked closet door I'd listened to my parents go at it, yelling and accusing one another. There were many times where the thinness of my walls felt like the only thing keeping me from being torn in half, each wanting me to bear witness to the other's transgressions. I reached into the bag for some Black Cats and the book of matches. I lit one and threw it. One of the guys from the other group came over and asked if he could have a couple. He took them back to the mermaid and stuck them into her breasts and lit the wicks. An explosion of sand rained down on them as they rolled around laughing.

"God, I miss the ocean," M said.

"Never been."

"Never?" she said. "When I was inside, one of my biggest fears was that I'd never see it again." She stood up, took off her shorts and tank top, and stood before me in her black bikini, removing a hair-tie so that her dreads fell down her shoulders. I have seen beautiful women since, but that image is burned on my brain. "How come you never go in the water with me?"

"You know why," I said.

Before long the other group took off in their houseboat, which left the beach silent but for the slow lapping of the water. I sat there a long time throwing the occasional Black Cat, watching M float on her back. The water stretched far into the distance, the same way the Missouri river did when I looked at it from the bridge where my father jumped or slipped. No note, we were never certain. I was sixteen when it happened. He'd stormed out after a fight with Mom. When he didn't come home that first night, we assumed he was sleeping it off somewhere as he sometimes did. But the next day the Yugo was found near the Broadway Bridge. It wasn't until the third day that his body finally surfaced twenty miles outside of the city in a man's fishing hole.

It was still cloudy when M walked out of the lake and sat down beside me. A cool breeze blew off the water, as small waves broke right at the shore. The sky was so hazy now that you could look straight at the sun. It sat above us, orange as a harvest moon, waiting to drop at any moment and end everything. I went to the boat to get the food and drinks we brought with us as well as a couple blankets. I stepped through the broken mermaid, crumpled by the wake, and water ran loose sand over my toes. The boat we rented from Bob had a small covered sleeping area, but it was so warm that night that we stayed on the beach. We lay in the sand sipping longnecks and watching fireworks destroy the sky above us until our eyes shut.

The Morning After the Morning After

I had to pull over for gas about an hour outside the city, using all but a couple bucks to fill half a tank. M got out of the car and went inside to use the bathroom. When she returned, she had a bottle of water and a gigantic pickle worthy of a ribbon at the county fair. Next to the gas station was a place called GIRLZ WORLD, with pictures of near-nude women draped over bubbly red writing: *Couples Welcome, Protecting Your First Amendment Rights!* Twenty yards away, near the highway, there was a billboard that showed a cherubic newborn under the heading *Thank You For "Choosing" Life.* I thought of the clinic. There was no baby inside

M's stomach and we were going to the clinic just as a precaution. This is what I told myself.

That Sunday had a sense of the elegiac about it: The Shermans would be arriving home soon, secreting away food they didn't want people to know about; I would head to my apartment to scan the want ads; and M would return to the record store, trying to feel better about being back in the world. Moving forward in our lives necessitates the continuous enactment of conclusions. We are, in fact, always and forever ending.

MY GOOD SIDE REALLY LIKES YOU

"Here we are," I said, looking at the clinic. We were sitting in the car across the street.

"There it is."

"Does it take long? Whatever it is they do?"

"No, not very," she said. "Just a pill."

Then we were quiet and neither of us moved from the car. The sky was beautiful and it felt good knowing it would be light out until nearly nine.

"Well," I said.

"You're not coming with me?"

"I don't do well in places like that," I pointed. "They're not my ideal environment."

"Well mine either, but Jesus, Steve," M said. "Are you actually going to make me go in there alone?" I quietly gripped the steering wheel, staring straight ahead. I could feel it coming, the way you sometimes sense the ominous. "Well, if you don't have the balls to come in, give me the money at least. Hand it over."

Hand it over? I thought. Where the fuck do you get off asking me for more money? Suddenly all fear and anxiety flushed from my heart and there was only the calm of anger guiding me. As we yelled at one another, I wasn't thinking about my girlfriend M, the parolee who woke up in the middle of the night with cold sweats and her eyes on fire. I was thinking about my empty wallet and how until that point, if I ever did have a baby, I'd been the kind of man I'd never want my child to know.

I don't remember much of what was said and I don't suppose it matters, because truth wasn't our objective; we wanted only to hurt each other.

"Don't have my baby!" I yelled.

"I won't—it'd probably be a loser just like you!"

We fought until there were no more words and she could only muster weakly, "Take me home, you asshole." And so I drove.

We fought often, almost from the day we met. After the first time, we made up by having quick, furious sex. Afterwards M said, "You need to understand, something's wrong with me. It's important you know this. Between prison and drugs, things don't connect anymore." She pointed at her head. "It's all screwed up." The grace of that moment is something I can barely comprehend and seems impossible to rise to. This time, however, there was no makeup. When we arrived at her mother's house in Overland Park, our contempt for one another draped over the car like a faulty parachute. She reached for the door and before she got out I asked what was happening.

"I don't know," she said. "I'm getting out of the car."

"How do you feel about me?"

"My good side really likes you. I think you're a good guy."

"And the bad? Does it hate me?"

"No." She paused. "It doesn't care."

CONFLUENCE

The Shermans weren't home yet. I punched the code and went inside to find a Mesozoic pile of dog shit fossilized on their largest oriental. I made no attempt to clean it up. At that moment I hated everything about the Shermans: their mansion and luxury cars, their paintings and antique furniture, their country club memberships and church donations. I took garbage bags down to the basement and began piling all the food I could fit into them. I looked up the staircase at the light above me, expecting the Shermans to arrive at any moment, but all I saw was Sally's head bobbing there. I loaded everything into the car. There have been times when I've felt so intensely that junk seemed like the only way to be in the world. I swear if I'd had money then I would have driven to the Paseo, but instead my car guided me to my mom's house in Brookside.

I began lugging the bags of food onto the porch, making a commotion. My mother opened the door and squinted into the dark. "Stephen?" she said. "What are you doing here?" I couldn't speak. I bent forward to hug her and then dropped to my knees, wrapping my arms around her waist. My mother. My cheek lay flat against her stomach. She asked what was wrong. "Are you high right now? I will call the police if I have to—for your own good." I told her what was in the bags and she began shaking. "Stealing from my friends? You *are* on drugs again!" My mother was crying now, repeating, "Why? Why, Stephen?" Even if I could have spoken at that moment, I wouldn't have been able to give her an answer. I didn't know why I did the things I did; that was the problem. I couldn't hold her anymore and stood up. As I began to step away, she pulled me close and whispered so softly that her breath on my cheek and ear felt like a kiss.

I drove around the city for hours that night, feeling alone and guilty. Finally, I stopped, pulling off into an empty lot near the confluence of the Kansas and Missouri rivers. I walked onto the Broadway Bridge, carrying the zoning flags M and I had stolen. It was as I stood there in the middle of the bridge, dumping the flags into the water below me that the sirens sounded and the lights flashed, reflecting blue and red off the dark water. My mom had called the police. Afterwards, when the cop knew I was clean, he could only cite me for petty theft. I didn't go to jail like M. I went home to my apartment, a little further in debt.

The thing I'd only started to realize on the bridge was that I'd lost two women that night. In my mind M and my mother are connected and sometimes bleed into one another. I saw M once or twice more before we fully quit on each other, but I haven't seen her in the nearly ten years since. I like to think she went to Peru when her parole was up and found Hector, that they started a family and farm. As for Mom, I sometimes still drive by the old house. The shame is that we'd never been able to communicate our true selves to one another. As I idle in the street next to her parked car, however, there's always a half-formed hope that she will appear in her bedroom window and begin moving her arms slowly and clearly through the air—skywriting—and maybe then we can start to understand. But then I hear her voice, those last words she spoke in my ear that night on the porch, and I begin to drive away: "You are not my son. You are not my son."

The Agriculture Hall of Fame

*There is a "scary" component to the birth process in horses—
a lot of things can go wrong, and when they do, they do in a
big way, dramatically, with no apparent regard for the tenu-
ous hold the new baby has on life. It is a powerful, dramatic,
and potentially violent event. Even though most foalings
occur successfully without external assistance, the birth of a
foal is potentially dangerous for both mare and foal because
it is such a paradox of powers—a David and Goliath story.*

KAREN HAYES, *The Complete Book of Foaling*

25_____Together they walked out into the midmorning light
and it felt like walking out of the old summer matinees of her childhood, the world surprising her with its presence. It put her in a mood
to wander, or linger rather, and instead of getting in the car to head
back to El Dorado she led him around town. Earlier, as she exited off
I-70, she'd seen a sign along the highway for a hotel still twenty miles
on yet that said "How About Doing Some Time in Leavenworth?" and
had a cartoon man in black and white prison clothes chained to a
bed. It made her think of her job, the dread of returning the following
morning. She wasn't ready to leave yet; she was hungry and wanted
something to eat. Stopped on a street corner, she looked at him and he
nodded, silent, and they continued walking.

At the Waffle House, as she watched him dip the corner of his toast into the runny yolk, she felt tired and thought they might stay the night and drive back home in the morning. To *their* home—the idea was still new to her. They would drive on to Leavenworth, go to that hotel she'd seen the sign for, and get a room. And that night they would order in, maybe drink a few shooters of bourbon, and then she'd bring in her camcorder from the car and play the tape of Arion's birth for him. And as the grainy pictures materialized, the struggle for life playing out quietly against the pale white wall of the room, maybe then it would make sense, it would feel okay, and she could pull him close and whisper all she'd never been able to say.

23_____The highway billboards and radio towers caught the periphery of her vision, appearing momentarily and then disappearing again. It was early and the dew beaded in lachrymal drops across the fields along I-70. Bonner Springs was a tiresome drive from El Dorado, and when they finally neared, a sign as tall as a water tower announced their arrival: The Agriculture Hall of Fame. She parked and paid their admission to a sleepy-eyed teenager in a blue vest before walking into the mostly empty building. Throughout the museum there were displays detailing the agricultural innovations of America over the last two hundred years. Meg milled through the decades with Jerry at her side, stopping once to regard Harry Truman's plow, until she found what she was looking for in the present-day display area. There were two photographs under the heading "The Agrarian Struggle." They were before-and-after pictures that Jerry had taken of farmland that had been bought by a rubber company and developed into a manufacturing plant. In the lower right hand corner she spied the credit: photographs courtesy of Jerry Curtis. Meg waited for the moment of recognition to cross his face, looking at the pictures and then over at him, half expecting this would be the cure. But there was nothing. He stood there with a calm look on his face, not a smile, but like he was pleased enough to be there, in that spot, at that moment. She wanted to turn to him and tell him that these were his photos, but when she looked over again he had already begun walking away.

20—————————"You're coming to stay with me for a while," she said.

"Hell I am."

Meg zipped up her purse and turned around in her chair. Jerry was standing close, looking down at her.

"Your doctor called me, Jerry." He took a step back. "Said you stormed out of his office."

"Leave me be, would you," he said, slowly lowering himself onto the couch.

"He tried calling, but your phone's been disconnected," she said. He looked like an obstinate child slouching in a pew on Sunday morning. "You listed me as your contact person. He told me."

19—————————The door had fallen into disrepair, cracks fissuring through the ancient lacquer. She knocked for a good five minutes, calling his name, before she heard the pull of the chain and the lock turning over. They met eyes for a few seconds in silence. His stubble had grown into a short, patchy beard. It made him look older, more than his forty-three years. He was wearing a pair of jeans and an opened button-down shirt. His eyes looked like he'd either been sleeping or drinking.

"Meg," he said finally with a touch of surprise. She was smiling and it felt good to look at her face.

"Hey, Jerry."

He moved aside from the door so she could come in. She walked past him into the dirty one-bedroom. She'd never been to his apartment before—he always came to visit her.

"How is your ankle?" she asked.

He looked down at his feet, wondering why she'd asked, and then back at her. "Fine, I suppose."

"Haven't seen you for a while. I tried calling, but you never answered, and then later it said your number wasn't in service anymore."

He finally shut the door, taking pains to turn the lock and put the chain back on, before turning to face her.

She looked around the room: sink full of dishes, mail piled on the kitchen table, newspapers and clothes strewn everywhere.

"Is everything okay?" she said.

"Of course. Just busy. Work and all."

"Work," she nodded. "I see."

She walked over to the kitchen and turned on the faucet. "Do you have any soap?"

"What are you doing?" he said. "Don't do that, Meg. Please."

She bent down, coming upon a near empty bottle of dish soap underneath the sink, and squirted some into the stream of warm water and bubbles began to foam. Jerry moved over and leaned against the wall. "What are you doing?" he repeated.

"Lending a hand, is all. From the looks of things you could certainly use it," she said, placing a dish in the dry rack. "Filthy in here. Like a hog in his sty."

After she finished the dishes, she picked up the newspapers and put his clothes in the hamper while Jerry trailed behind her, complaining step for step. It struck him as rude. He didn't come to her house and start rearranging things. For a while she let herself believe that there wasn't anything wrong (he was a messy man, if ever she'd seen one), but what told her otherwise was sitting down to sort the mail and seeing the bills that hadn't been paid in months.

"What are you doing?" he said yet again.

She turned to look at him.

"Why haven't you paid these?" she said, holding up a fistful of envelopes from utility companies.

"Those are wrong. They overcharged me. I've got to call them." She put the bills into her purse and he felt an anger pass through him, that he hadn't hidden it better, that she was finding out this way, that she couldn't just let him be. "What the hell do you think you're doing?" He fulminated: "Just leave me alone!"

She stood there silently steadfast, still.

Jerry sat in a chair, put his head in his hands, and began to speak quietly. Meg realized he was counting. She wondered what he was doing—"fourteen, thirteen, twelve"—but let him continue until he could no longer count, shaking so bad.

16_____ After the vet came out for a final visit, giving her a window of time in which the labor would happen, Meg used almost all of her vacation time at work. It was on her fourth day off when Pallas went into labor and she called Shoal at two in the morning. "It's happening," she told him. There was a pause as he muffled the phone, and then he said he'd be there in twenty minutes. He had to drive from the other side of town because he lived in one of the new developments where a lot of the Wichita commuters settled.

Meg hung up and walked back to the barn. She double- and triple-checked her supplies and loaded the camera with batteries and switched on the power.

Pallas's outer placenta tore, breaking the water, while she was waiting for Shoal, so she wrapped Pallas's tail and washed her vulva and udder, as she had seen her mother do years before when she watched from the barn loft, both excited and terrified. Shoal arrived a few minutes later and stood regarding her silently, as though trying to cook up an excuse to leave. She dropped the sponge in the bucket and dried her hands before giving him the camera. He stood behind it with his eye in the viewfinder, following Meg's every move. "Like this?" he asked. She was bent over Pallas, who was on her side, limbs strewn along the floor of her stable.

"Not me," she said to him, "stay on Pallas." She could tell Shoal was tense—the way he began sniffling—as she reached her gloved hand into the vulva to guide the foal out. There was a dank, pungent odor and she could hear Shoal breathing out of his mouth.

The whole process took only fifteen minutes. Twelve months for fifteen minutes. She'd always thought it a necessary balancing on nature's part that though the length of a mare's term was three months longer than a woman's, the foaling often happened very quickly. When the muzzle appeared, Meg ripped the white amnion away and stripped out the nostrils. It was a beautiful thing seeing dam and foal lie together, his hind limbs still in the mare's vagina, connected.

A tradition begun years ago, her parents always favored mythological names and she would call him Arion. There was a dog-eared copy of a book she kept by her bed that had been her mother's, filled with the Greek and Roman stories she'd listened to as a child before bed. Every night she'd huddle under the thick quilt her grandmother had stitched while her mother sat in the hardwood chair, speaking in a soft manner, almost whispering—not with the flare of a storyteller, but of someone saying something important. It was with this book that her mother would pick out the names used for identifying the stock. Given all the animals that had passed through the farm over the years there were few names that hadn't been used at some point. She'd developed attachments to certain names, too, and had begun to use them repeatedly. This Pallas was her third. But for this birth she wanted something special, something she'd never used before. She'd come across it while perusing the index of the mythology book and was amazed they'd never seen it before. Next to the names were terse notes of identification. She couldn't recall this one from any of the stories. Beside Arion it said: *Greek poet and musician; also name of first horse.*

In the hour after the birth, as the fluid drained from the colt's lungs, he attempted walking several times, his young legs initially failing to suffer the weight. Shoal, yawning, asked if they were through. "Keep filming," she said, but as Pallas passed the afterbirth and Meg began separating it, submerging it in water to take to the vet for testing, Shoal became sick. She walked him to his car. There was a soft light hovering from the sickle moon overhead.

"I'm sorry," he said.

"Kind of intense, isn't it," she grinned.

"Yeah," he said, getting into his old, yellow Chevelle. "You're going to tell everyone at work that I couldn't hack it, aren't you?" He smiled as he retrieved keys from the pocket of his jeans and slid one into the ignition. "A marine couldn't watch a horse give birth," he laughed once, exhausted.

She shook her head, calmly smiling. "Thank you for being here, Shoal," she said, and slowly walked back to the barn, where from the shadows she filmed the first few hours of mother and child getting to know one another.

15_____ Meg had a system for the whole thing. She wanted to deliver the foal herself, but she needed help. She had tried calling Jerry, but there had been no answer and she couldn't bring herself to leave a message, looking so desperate. She wanted someone strong in case she needed help lifting foal or dam, so she asked one of the guards from the prison where she worked, a black man named Shoal. He'd worked there since coming back from Desert Storm and she'd heard stories about him, that once he wrestled an inmate to the floor who'd pulled a crude knife from his sock. When she asked him about it later, he'd just smiled and said, "Who told you that?" It was fair to say they were friendly, but she wondered if she was crossing a line.

"Help you how?" he said when she brought it up. She was filling her mug with coffee in the break room, preparing to head back to administration where a stack of files awaited processing. Shoal worked the day shift, so they often passed one another when she arrived for work in the morning, exchanging small talk before he'd head through the rolling steel bars to the other side of the prison, where the inmates were. Now he was sipping the last bit of coffee from his cup and the stale, oaky smell of his breath traveled between them.

"I want you to film this for me. The foaling. Do you know how to use a camera?"

He looked a little surprised, then confused. She realized her brain was moving too fast, forgetting he hadn't thought about this for the many hours she had, that this was in fact the first wind he was catching of her plan, and so the look on his face was akin to someone having been proposed to at the end of a first date, rushing color and warmth to Meg's cheeks. "Reckon so," he mumbled, adding cream to his cup.

"I'll be busy helping with the—" she started, but could see the doubt still in his eyes. She realized how strange this must seem and wanted to turn and leave, but then she was speaking: "Please, it's important to me. Won't you help?"

Shoal put the cream down, threw away the stirring stick, and met her eyes.

13_____Later, after a long, quiet drive back to his apartment, Jerry remembered going to see his grandfather as a boy and sitting there with the old man as his father spoke. There was never a name for what was wrong with him, other than the wear of old age, but it made sense now. Sometimes the old man would respond to questions, but periodically he'd lapse into long silences, and when he would finally look up and make eye contact with Jerry or his father, there was something in his eyes—not the look of someone struggling to remember, but the warm gleam of someone intrigued by something unfamiliar, something new.

12_____"You've been doing great, Jerry," his doctor said. He had done away with the formalities after a handful of appointments. His overly chipper exclamations had grown on Jerry in the way one warms to something he thinks is beneath him, like a hokey song or silly trend. They were in a different examination room this time; it was darker and there were flat rectangular lights all over the walls for viewing x-rays and scans. Jerry sat on the edge of a table, his legs dangling like a child's, the pressure from which was building behind his knees. His doctor held up a large sheet of film to one of the lights.

"Hmm," he said.

"See something in there, Doc? Ain't but some clouds to this eye."

"Well, see here, Jerry," he said, turning back toward him and circling part of the picture. "This is what I'm concerned about." He handed it to Jerry and was beginning to say something, when his pager sounded and he excused himself from the room.

Jerry was covered in the same revealing smock they always had him wear, and he sat on the examination table looking at the film, following the doctor's shaky pencil. He couldn't even tell what part of his body was in the picture; it seemed they'd scanned every inch of him, looking for answers. The doctor's marking didn't seem to note anything abnormal, but who the hell knew. There was nothing like Jerry so often heard described—a growth—some malignancy springing up unwanted. The doctor had left the pictures in a pile on the table, and Jerry picked them up and moved them around in the light. The one in his hand, a color picture, looked as pink as a litter of newborn piglets. It was from one of the slew of tests he'd finally relented to after his request for a quick fix of pills was denied. "How can I prescribe medication if I don't know what I'm prescribing for?" his doctor had said, smiling. These pictures were ambiguous and uncertain, unlike the ones development companies hired him to take that were so clear and understandable, well defined like the even tracts of Kansas land that were his subjects. His photos, taken from helicopters, were used by companies to survey and plan the building of their manufacturing plants or professional buildings, occasionally the clichéd strip mall or parking lot. It wasn't always steady work, but it paid well and he'd been doing it so long he always got called first for a job.

He put the pictures down and sat still, staring at his feet, remembering when his ankle had swollen some months ago and Meg had taken him in and fixed him supper. *Meg*, he was thinking when the doctor came back in, apologizing.

"What about it? What's it mean?" Jerry said, pointing at the photo with the marking on it.

The doctor stopped to compose himself. "Well those are plaques, Jerry." He pulled out a pen from his pocket and pointed at the CAT scan. "See, this is a scan of your brain, and these gray spots are plaques—"

"You telling me I should've been at the dentist all this time?"

The doctor seemed unsure whether he should laugh or not, then said: "No, no. You're in the right place." He clicked his pen once. "Jerry, I believe they are responsible for the problems you've been having." He let this sink in. Jerry ran a finger over one of the scans. "Your memory problems."

Jerry looked at him and scoffed, "Shit, who doesn't have those? Just a little confused. I'm getting old," he added, meaning it to be a joke because at forty-three he still felt pretty damn good, only the doctor wasn't smiling.

"Sure, to a degree some memory loss is normal with age, but the kind of loss I'm talking about, and the kind of loss you've been experiencing, is abnormal."

The stiffness behind his knees was getting worse. He could feel his leg beginning to fall asleep, so he shifted his weight, moving around his rear on the table. Memory, sure. For some time, a couple years maybe. It embarrassed him. There had been small things at first, going blank on familiar names and phone numbers, forgetting to pick up the mail. Nothing too alarming, but then he forgot to show up for a job in Hutchinson and was fired, costing him a lot of money, several months' rent on his apartment in Gardner. That was when he knew something was wrong. It was hard to admit that he had to pick up the paper several times a day to help remember what day it was—not that he didn't know. He did, really, but a slow creeping doubt often held him in a fog of uncertainty.

"These plaques are rare in someone your age," his doctor continued. "That's why we've had to put you through so many tests." Jerry squinted. "We don't usually see the onset until someone's sixties or seventies."

The word was floating around the room, but no one was going to be the first to say it. For a moment he wanted to make a scene, scream, *Not me, there's been a mix up of charts—second opinion*. But he knew.

"Like I said, it's rare but not unheard of. Especially if there is evidence of it in the past. The disease is largely hereditary. You haven't indicated this, the family history portion of your chart says nothing, but—"

"You telling me I'm gonna forget everything?"

He looked at the pictures beside him. He hated having everything inside him on display. All those photos of different parts of his body separated from one another, unconnected. And now he saw that soon his gossamer memories would continue to thin and he'd be alone.

His doctor was writing out prescriptions and talking at a speed that made Jerry's eyes glaze over. "Do you have someone to help you at home? You only list one person on your contact sheet. Meg Wilson, is she family?" His doctor was telling him he would die alone, confused and terrified, but not telling him. Of course, there was medication that would help, he said. What he wasn't saying was that there was no cure.

He was telling Jerry about exercises he should be doing every day, reciting loved one's ages and birthdays, making daily lists, always wearing a watch with the time and date. One in particular he recommended was numbers, counting down from twenty-five before bed and each morning. "Think of it as exercise. Like pushups for your brain," he said, trying to muster a smile. The doctor was speaking as he wrote in the chart when Jerry stood up and took off his one-piece, standing there naked in front of the doctor, who, after an awkward moment, turned his back to Jerry and began talking again. Jerry put on his jeans, shirt, and boots, and left the room. The doctor followed him out, waving a fistful of prescriptions like betting stubs, calling Jerry's name.

10_____The barn was wide open, so she heard everything. From the eleventh month on she'd taken to sleeping out there. By late September it was starting to get cool at night, so she slept in sweatpants on top of bales of hay with a thick wool blanket covering her. Several of the nameless barn cats that gravitated to the farm stayed with her. She could hear them walking along the crossbeams of the drafty barn. Sometimes she'd wake, alarmed by a noise, staring into their ghostly eyes. As Pallas's cycle neared its twelve-month revolution, Meg found herself more and more excited, expectant, and nervous. She wanted to deliver the foal herself. She never had; she'd always just called the vet to do it, but something struck her now, this feeling of last chance.

It had been months since she'd last seen Jerry. His birthday had passed and her call went unreturned, her card unanswered. She thought often about their night together and wanted to call and say something, anything, but she couldn't bring herself to pick up the phone. And still it lingered: this thought, or hope even, that one day they would get it right.

8_____They put him in a tube and told him not to move. Then they had to do it again, and then one more time after that. The doctor had told him this was one of the standard tests, but it made Jerry uncomfortable. "Remember, you can't move," he said. "Try to stay as still as possible, so that we can get the clearest reading we can. If you don't, then we'll have to do it again." He said this with a forced smile and show of perfectly straight, white teeth that seemed to say *Don't mess it up like you did last time, hick* and nodded to the lab technician, who hit the button that sent Jerry, prostrate, back into the bright tunnel. There was an itch on his leg and Jerry wanted more than anything to scratch it. Without tilting his head, he tried to pinpoint the exact location of the itch. He was naked except for the little one-piece the nurse had given him. They said he could have a headset to listen to the radio while he was inside, but he told them he'd prefer not to. Now the claustrophobic silence of the tube struck him more and more like a coffin, and there was only his heartbeat, which pulsed away incessantly, as though trying to extinguish a lifetime's allotment of beats. Don't move, he thought, trying to picture the exact location of the itch, squinting, but could already hear the doctor shouting "One more time" to the technician behind the glass.

7_____That night they made love in the huge bed that had been Meg's parents', metal posts pushing into age-old divots in the oak floor. Jerry smelled as he always did, as he always would, Meg thought. Some mixture of dried sweat and musk aftershave that she'd come to associate with strength and loss.

He had shown up at the farm nearly fifteen years ago, when Meg had taken it over from her dead parents. He'd come in response to an ad for temporary help he'd seen in the paper during a slow period in his own work. At that point she'd gone through a slew of itinerants who'd work for a week or two, sometimes not lasting the day, before disappearing into one of El Dorado's many bars. Jerry, though, ended up staying on for three months, helping Meg with the farm before going back to taking photographs for land developers. Without acknowledging so, the two had grown close, maintaining on the surface a confrontational rapport that was tempered by unspoken care and support. By the end of those three months at the farm he'd moved from the guesthouse into her bedroom. In the still mornings they'd quietly rise, naked, and dress as she readied to leave for her job at the prison and he to the list of tasks she left for him on the kitchen table. When she returned in the evening, they would feed the animals together, walking in step across the grounds, and afterwards she'd fix supper. And then sometime later, without warning, he'd begin to unbutton her blouse or reach his arms around her, maybe as she washed the dishes, and breathe into the slope of her neck, the stubble of his chin shooting a chilled tingle through her limbs.

She knew he'd been with many women, that he was in fact the kind of man infidelity and restlessness seemed to emanate from, but it didn't much matter to her then. She'd fallen hard for him, but when a job opened up that he couldn't turn down he'd left despite her, saying he'd return now and again. And he did, now and again. He visited periodically, dropping in unexpectedly every month or two. This was the way things were with them, and she would have to be content or move on. There would always be jobs and other women he'd be running away to, and he would never be able to settle down. Worst of all, she had never brought herself to tell him what was most difficult, that two months after he left, those terrifying sixty days of waiting for either him to call or her period to arrive, she made the short drive from El Dorado to Wichita alone.

She'd allowed the years to confuse whether she'd made that silent drive to the clinic out of spite for him or personal doubt, and now there was just this horrible guilt, for both not telling Jerry and for the oft-dreamed child. She wanted to whisper it in his ear now, in bed, as she pulled him tight against her and looked into the deep brown of his eyes. But as he moved inside her, a soft, slow rhythm against her thighs, they came together, and she said nothing. Afterwards, Jerry held her, and they listened to the cicada sound through the night, thinking. Jerry knew it was time to settle down, while Meg just wanted to wake up next to him. But when she felt him slipping out of bed and heard him inching down the stairway in the predawn quiet, she feigned sleep. She let him go, hearing the engine rattle and finally turn over, because this was the way things were.

6_____She saw Jerry's pickup arrive after the sun sank on the horizon, pulling the mauve sky toward blackness. She had made her final rounds and was heading back to the house after feeding Hephaestus and Mercury, the last of her calves.

She was not surprised by Jerry's visit; this was his way, to show up unannounced. She waved to him as he got out of his red pickup. He limped out of cab and followed her around back, then up the steps to the kitchen door. "What have you done to yourself?" she said, nodding at his leg.

"Usual stuff."

"The usual stuff for someone who hangs out of helicopters, you mean." He grinned at her. "Come on, let me fix you something," she said. He followed her inside, slowly moving up the steps and through the door.

"Place looks nice, Meg," he said. She'd moved some things around since his last visit.

"You're a good liar," she smiled over her shoulder. She was washing her hands at the sink. "How long's it been? Four months?" He shrugged. "Been waiting for you to come around again. Got a whole list of doings I could use your help with." She dried her hands on a terrycloth towel hanging from the stove handle. "I'm trying to hold this place together, but I wake up each morning half expecting to find myself buried underneath it." They both laughed. "I swear if someone came by and made an offer . . . Who knows, someday maybe you'll be in the air taking pictures of this place, so someone can just bulldoze it—turn it into something new, like everywhere else." She had meant this lightheartedly but regretted it, sensing the awkwardness it brought into the room. Jerry snorted a single conciliatory laugh.

"I can help," he said, leaning back and putting his bum ankle up on an empty chair.

"Don't fool yourself. I saw the way you limped in here. You're either getting old or you hurt yourself. Well, which is it?" He thought back to the previous night when he'd gone home with that young gal from the bar, so drunk she tried to pull her jeans off over her boots and fell to the floor. All through it she alternated between giggling and moaning and afterwards rolled off of him and passed out. Jerry got up to go to the bathroom and banged his shin against the side of his bed and fell to the ground, rolling his ankle. He'd yelled a string of cuss words but the girl was so gone she only shuddered in her sleep. He lay on the floor, feeling a starry lightheadedness accompany the pain. Within the hour his ankle had swollen into a purple softball.

Meg looked at him with his feet up on the chair. She still found herself wildly attracted to him, old as he looked limping around. He had a strong build, a chest like an overturned canoe. His dark hair was just beginning to salt, and his face was creased with years of hard work but could easily charm the strongest willed. Her mother used to say men like Jerry had a lot of devil in their eyes.

Jerry didn't want to think about the night before, or his ankle, or his trips to the doctor, all those tests. No answers. It felt good seeing Meg again, being around her. It always felt good, every time he came back. "You've grown your hair out," he said. Her back was to him, looking out the window, and he liked the way the hair snaked around her ears, still a soft reddish brown. The spring brought out the faint red streaks. "I don't suppose there's a man here that I'm making wildly jealous, is there?"

"You wouldn't make a horny toad jealous. Besides, you know me." She turned away, reaching for a sack of potatoes she kept above the stove.

"Yeah, I know you," he snorted. "Suppose the only men I have to compete with are those calves I saw you tending to."

"I like being alone," she said quickly, and then wished she hadn't sounded so defensive. She was peeling potatoes now and warming the skillet. "That's Mercury and Hephaestus," she said, turning on the faucet.

"Your names," he said. "They them Demeter calved?" Jerry said, but Meg didn't hear him over the din of water that washed peels from her hands into the disposal. She shut the water off. "How is old Demi?" he raised his voice.

"Heifer's gone." She paused, drying her hands. "Gone mad is more like it, though. After she bore those two out there," Meg said, motioning outside with the tilt of her chin, "she took to madness." Meg dumped a handful of potatoes into a silver mixing bowl and added cream and salt. "She beat on them, her own kids—kicking them. I didn't know what to do. If I let her be, she would have killed them, that much I was sure of. I loved that old girl, but I knew I could still get something for her on the market, so I sold her. Lord knows I needed the money."

Jerry enjoyed watching Meg move around a kitchen she was so familiar with. Earlier that evening she had laid out a large steak to defrost for dinner. It would have lasted two meals anyway, so she cut it in half and put the two smaller steaks on the skillet, then turned around to face him, a keen rush filling her. "You know what though? Pallas's gonna foal. She's nearly halfway along."

"That's good," he grinned at her excitement. "Gonna have a little one around here."

She turned back toward the stove. "I hope. Hasn't happened in a long while, since I had to sell most of the stock. So few of them anymore." She stabbed one of the steaks with a fork, sending a sibilant hiss throughout the kitchen. "Mama used to help with the birth. I remember watching, just a scared little girl. Seemed like magic that she could help a living thing come out of such a violent mess."

"Blood, shit, and piss," Jerry nodded.

"Death, too," Meg added, speaking over her left shoulder. "We lost a few, I remember." She adjusted the flame of the burner under the skillet. "I'm gonna do this one myself. Deliver the foal. I could use your help." He said sure, he supposed he could, but Meg knew it was nothing to depend upon. Fifteen years and you learn a thing or two about a person, about expectations.

"Ares sired then?"

"He's the daddy alright. Must have happened right before I sold him," she said.

"You sold Ares?" he said, thinking back on the large stallion he helped break.

"Needed the money, Jer. Things aren't what they used to be. As Daddy would say, the business ain't."

"So there's no one else? No more horses?"

"Pallas's all," she said. "And that baby inside her."

They were quiet a minute and there was only the crackle of the cooking steaks.

"You still clerking out at the prison?" he finally said.

"Sure am. Makes the days come and go." She flipped the steaks over. "You still take yours medium?"

He grunted in affirmation.

"And you. Still picture-taking?"

"Pays the bills," he nodded. His leg was getting stiff and he adjusted his ankle, asking if she had a beer or something. She apologized for not having offered and went to the fridge, where she grabbed a bottle, twisted off the top, and set it before Jerry. He took a sip and sat there rotating the brown bottle slowly in circles, thinking about the last appointment he'd had with the doctor, still no answers, and whether he should tell Meg. No, he thought, not now. "You know it's funny though. I got a letter the other day from the Hall of Fame."

"The what?"

"The Agriculture Hall of Fame."

"You did," she said over her shoulder. "Lord, what for?"

"They say they want to use some of my photos in an exhibit."

"No they didn't." She turned to face him, smiling. "Why?" Sometimes around him she found herself as ebullient and coy as a crushing sixteen-year-old.

"I swear," he said, shaking his head. "Something about a display. They got my name from a developer I worked for once, I reckon." He thought about all the pictures he'd taken over the years, all those farms that had been turned into something else, that no longer existed. It was more pleasant than the present; he hadn't worked in a month. "I mean, I don't know what the display will be, but the thing is, they want my pictures. In a museum." He felt a little foolish for placing such significance on the modest honor. But the truth was he did feel proud.

He shook his head. "You'll come see them, won't you?"

"Where is it?"

"Not quite to Leavenworth. Bonner Springs."

"Together," she said, then affirmed: "We'll go together."

She switched on the mixer, adding a little more cream and salt to the potatoes, and the room echoed with the buzz. He studied the outline of her shoulders hidden beneath her shirt.

"Now make sure you don't burn that steak, girl."

She loved when he spoke like that.

"Hush up now, I know just the way you like it."

4_____Jerry looked around the doctor's office and wanted to leave. He had come to the hospital as a last resort. Pain was something he had learned to live with his whole life (wasn't much aspirin couldn't fix), but lately was different. Not pain so much. Something in his head. He was sitting in the room on a table that was covered with what seemed to be butcher paper and made an awful sound whenever he moved. All around him on the walls were posters of smiling people. Jerry was nettled about not being able to find a specialist in Gardner, having to drive clear out to Kansas City.

The doctor would be in in a few minutes, the nurse had said after taking Jerry's vitals and showing him to the examination room. The prick showed up twenty minutes later.

There was nothing to like about him: the white coat he'd so starched it barely reacted to his movements; the shiny gold pens in his pocket; his manner of speaking, the way he seemed to end every sentence with an exclamation point; his gelled hair; the way he walked in looking at Jerry's chart, avoiding eye contact; and most of all his youth. What was this doctor going to tell him he didn't already know? This kid who didn't know his ass from a hole in the ground.

"So, tell me about your recent troubles, Mr. Curtis," he said, finally looking up, and his eyes seemed to almost sparkle.

3_____Every day when Meg left her shift at the prison she found herself driving down Main Street, noticing the people and storefronts the newly revitalized downtown had begun to attract to this small town in southeastern Kansas. She remembered as a girl hearing her grandfather speak of a time when El Dorado had been a booming oil town before the ground dried up and the companies moved their refineries to the western parts of the state, looking for untapped reserves. There were small towns surrounding El Dorado that had literally evaporated when those companies left. And after the oil craze, locals had turned to farming and ranching, shipping steer all across the country, but recent decades had seen most either consumed by large corporate farms or fold in bankruptcy. There were few family farms left, putting a drag of the local economy that depended upon them. The opening of the prison was supposed to mitigate these hits, ensuring an abundance of allocated state money, but with it came a shift in focus away from agriculture to industry and service. Now they were building everywhere, as though every inch of land had to be used for something other than its natural purpose. It made Meg uneasy. At what cost? she thought.

Her route home took her from the south end of El Dorado, near Wichita, past the northern limits into the rolling Flint Hills, where the roads became gravel and the native grass stretched to eye level as her car wound around and over small hillocks past grain silos and Quonset huts until her farm appeared over the crest of a final knoll. Initially, you only saw the farmhouse, but as the road curved around the small arc of hardwood trees, the barn and paddock became visible, as well as the guest house, which in her grandparents' and even her parents' times was referred to as the servant quarters, though they'd never really had servants, just workers—Indians, mostly—stealing off from the Oklahoma reservations, looking to make a few bucks. Sometimes her father took them on months at a time as extra hands or occasionally nannies and cooks when all the kids were still in the house. Now though, living alone and with no relative within a day's drive, Meg used the tumbledown building for storage.

Much of any prominence the farm had garnered died with her father. Afterwards, there was no one in the family willing or strong enough to regulate the horse and cattle trade so as to be profitable. Her brothers had left for separate coasts after college and her mother died shortly thereafter. Burdened both by a sense of nostalgia and obligation, Meg was the only one left fighting to keep the farm going. And she did fight, even if it meant an endless succession of problems and upkeep, not to mention financial strain and debt. Today her memories of a barn teeming with horses and scores of grazing cattle out to pasture were reduced to a couple of calves and one horse, her own: Pallas.

After a day at the prison, working in clerical, she would come home and make supper and then go out to feed her animals. Spring nights like this were her favorite, the warm breeze and the fading sunlight that seemed to take an eternity to set. Tonight she decided to skip dinner and changed right into jeans and a long-sleeve shirt, hurrying outside to see Pallas. She approached the barn and found her in the stable, lying in hay. Meg looked at her, studying her striking brown coat and long black mane, and thought she was the most beautiful creature she'd ever seen. And then she smiled, measuring the slight distension of Pallas's stomach. Weeks back she'd had a hunch and she saw now she had been right. She clicked her tongue and dropped a few peppermint treats. Pallas looked over at her, snorted, and then closed her eyes. "Hey, baby girl," Meg said. "You ready to be a mama?"

2_____ From above it all seemed so small and ordered: the way the land neatly divided into parallel tracts, the doll-sized simplicity of houses and buildings that looked like they'd never been disturbed, the sinuous roads, twisting but never desultory—always leading somewhere. "A little lower," Jerry yelled to John, who held the rope on Jerry's harness, the only failsafe against Jerry's swan dive to death, the long but hurried fall that would end in an undramatic thud amongst some poor farmer's spring crop. There was pain in Jerry's chest from John's firm pull on the harness. Jerry looked back at him and John eased his hold. Jerry inched out of the doorway further, trying to get the perfect shot. With the camera at his eye and the centrifugal drone of the helicopter's blades, he found himself thinking about Lana. He looked over his shoulder after snapping a couple of shots and saw her sitting there on the hard metal seat with her hands at her ears, hair blowing every which way, smiling nervously.

He grinned at her, a look with which he meant to say *Don't worry, little peach. I do this all the time.* She would surely be impressed with the skill Jerry displayed for the job, the flair that twenty-three years experience afforded. Even at forty-two he found himself pulling the same moves he had as a dumb, reckless kid.

She had been there waiting for him earlier in the day when he swung open the door of his red pickup truck, tawny with rust, at Anderson Industries, thirty minutes late. It was a job for a rubber factory, land they wanted to turn into a plant. She was wearing a matching violet pantsuit with black trim, which she'd probably bought for her first job after graduation. Her blond hair whispered around her cheek and neck, and as he approached she was holding a hand to her eye to block the sun. She liked him from the start. He could tell. She looked him over once, her eyes lingering on his faded blue jeans, white t-shirt, and arms.

"You're late," she said as they walked inside. "We were expecting you a half-hour ago, Mr. Curtis."

"You were, were you," he grinned. "If I'd known *you* were gonna meet me, I would have shown up last night." He scratched at his chin. "Call me Jerry."

These companies always seemed to have a gorgeous young girl, fresh out of school, to meet and to show him around and he enjoyed the challenge they presented: their novice professionalism and earnest pursuit of a job well done. On nights he spent alone in his apartment Jerry liked to muse about the ones he'd coaxed into sharing his bed; it helped him sleep when the loneliness came.

He looked at her as they walked inside the office building. She was trying to be all business, her achingly straight back and quick stride.

"What's your name, girl?" he asked.

She stopped sharply and turned to look at him, as though he'd tickled her ire, then said, "Lana," and a small smile formed on her lips. "Now if we do not get in the air soon, we'll both be looking for new jobs. This is John," she said, pointing to a large man slouching in a chair by the office. "He'll be going up with us to help you with your shots."

He watched her walk down the hallway, smiling at the way her body curved underneath her sleek suit when she moved with such purpose. "Lana," he called after her, his pitch going high as though he had something important to say. "What do you say we grab a bite to eat after this whole deal?" He continued watching her as the sound of her heels clopping against the floor provided percussion to the song playing inside his head.

Now in the helicopter he felt the security of John's grip holding him as he measured the land in the viewfinder, playing this game he sometimes did, thinking that only if he were taking the perfect picture would he get lucky tonight with Lana. He looked, focused the lens, sized up the area, and clicked.

John

His name was Barish and as we shook hands again, for the first time in several months, I could still smell the way he would pour on his cologne. Never to his face, I used to call it "the Turkish shower." He smiled and I smiled back, our hands locked. It was a surprisingly warm October evening, so we decided to sit on the deck of an off-campus bar that made its own beer, overlooking all of Wichita. It had been one of our favorite haunts when we lived together, but I hadn't been back since. The previous year we'd shared a cramped room in the honors dorm at Wichita State. It felt good to be in a familiar place with a familiar friend. He ordered a raspberry beer, the house special, and I ordered the heavy stout. A lot had changed since we last saw each other. He had graduated and was now in the first year of his master's in engineering. I was still an undergrad, a senior. We hardly saw each other anymore on campus, but he'd e-mailed me asking if I wanted to meet for a drink.

Beer spilled over the lip of his pint when he sat down.

"How's it going?" I said.

"Not bad, not bad," he shrugged, smiling. He had a tendency to repeat his answers during small talk. And smile. He was always smiling.

"How's the program?"

"It is shit. They forgot to pay me for month. For my research assistantship. A month, they forgot," he laughed, looking out at the city.

"I had to tell them to pay me my money. You do not want to mess with angry Turk." He slammed his fist against the table, spilling some of the head off my beer.

"Bastards," I said. I liked hearing Barish's voice again, the familiar accent and awkward inflection, dropped articles and possessives. The way he spoke English, the staccato-like emphasis on wrong syllables, made me think of someone standing on a partially frozen lake, hopping from safe spot to safe spot. We sat for a minute, meeting eyes. He looked thinner. He was tall and had dark skin and a large, broad nose. God, the nights I lay awake silently cursing his snoring. He used to put gel in his short black hair, so much so that it looked like wet papier-mâché, but now it had grown long and he pulled it back over his ears.

"How are your parents?" I asked.

He said they were good, that things were slowly beginning to recover. That previous year when we lived together Turkey was beset by horrible earthquakes. The economy nearly collapsed, and for a while he was really worried, thought he might even leave school. Barish was on the computer all the time, looking for updates on the situation. But things slowly got better and he stayed—his parents wanted him to, he said. What seemed to ease him during that time was listening to games of his favorite soccer team streaming on the Internet. He loved it, the game—everyone did over there, he said. He used to tell me how there were several deaths each year stemming from celebrations after soccer victories. Once, a stray bullet ricocheted off a building and hit a pregnant woman returning home from the market. A shame, he said, shaking his head. So I suppose it was fitting when that spring, with the country just beginning to recover, his team won the European Cup.

"I would like to get out of here though," he said, and raised a single finger. "Wichita is not for Turkish man."

I nodded and took a sip of my beer. "Back home?"

"Yes," he said, but shook his head no. "Most probably Kansas City. Sprint has big office. I will put my résumé there. My friend had internship and said good thing."

Then he waved his hand and said, "Enough business. How is girlfriend?"

"We broke up," I said quickly. "She dumped me."

"Fuck me sideways," he said solemnly. There were certain curse words and expressions he'd hear someone say in a movie or on the street that afterwards he'd repeat regardless of context or appropriate usage; I think he just liked the way certain words sounded.

"Yeah, she dumped me," I repeated, taking a sip of the bitter stout.

We'd been together since high school. She'd gone to college in Oregon and after nearly three years said we were too far apart, that it wasn't working. Barish used to tease me because I talked to her on the phone so much. It made me feel henpecked and ashamed that he thought I was needy, and worse because he was right.

"She was fucking some other guy," I lied.

"Bitch," he sneered. It was the first time the smile gave way. But he quickly shook it off. "She is not worth it, my man. Plenty fish in barrel," he said, smiling, extending an arm out to the rest of the deck as though expecting it to be suddenly full of beautiful women. But there were only two other people, a guy and girl, a couple, undergrads. "That is end of pussy-whipping for her," he consoled.

He shook his head again and we both finished our pints in long gulps.

"Another?" I said, beginning to rise from my chair.

"Please," he said, extending his hand so that I'd sit back down. "It is my obligation." He got up and went inside to order at the bar. I looked around the deck.

The young couple was getting up to leave. Happy Hour was ending. The girl wore shorts with the name of her sorority stitched across the butt. I watched them walk inside holding hands, and suddenly I wanted to yell something hurtful, though specifics failed me. Since the breakup I rarely went out anymore. I spent most nights in my efficiency ignoring paper assignments that had gotten me kicked out of the honors program, watching the twenty-four-hour news channels incessantly, and hating myself for entering and deleting the number of my ex's cell.

A minute later Barish appeared at the door and pushed it open with his foot, four beers clamped together in his hands. Though his name was Barish, he went by John because he'd seen a picture of JFK in the airport when he first landed in America and thought he was handsome. He said it was easier for people to pronounce, that he liked the sound of it, simple enough. He tried so hard to fit in. The first day we met, I'd lugged several heavy bags into my new dorm room to find him standing there smiling, right hand extended, the posters of James Dean and Marilyn Monroe already taped to the wall, looming over his shoulder. I was always trying to get him to keep his customs, telling him that people understood here, that we respected difference. But he insisted that this was his culture now, and he did love it, however out of touch with it he often was.

"What are those?" I asked as he put the pints down. I didn't recognize the hue.

"Is season special," he said, pushing two of them my way. "Has more alcohol." He took a sip and, as if determining from the taste, said, "Three percent more."

"Great," I said, taking a pull.

It was starting to get dark. The deck lights hadn't yet turned on, but I imagined any minute now. I thought of the coming winter months when, dark by four o'clock, it seemed as though you hardly saw the sun. We each finished a glass quickly, quietly.

Then he pulled a piece of paper from his pocket and leaned forward. "Have you seen?" Even though we were the only ones out there, he looked over his shoulder like we were cons splitting up the booty. He unfolded the paper and spun it around so I could see. It was a color picture he'd printed off his computer of a man having his picture taken on the observation deck of one of the towers. He had on a black jacket and was smiling, unaware of the plane, hidden in the corner of the picture, headed right for him.

"Shit," I said, pulling back from the table a little. "That's messed up. Is it real?"

He shrugged. "A friend sent me," he said, letting me look at it a few seconds longer before folding it back up. He made a move to put it in his pocket, then set it next to his beer.

Barish was a secular Muslim, but that meant little only weeks after the attack. It was that weird time when none of us could make sense of what had happened and we were willing to accept anything that might help us comprehend its largeness. The Internet was awash in conspiracy theories and explanations, and we clung to it all—whether the forged auguries of Nostradamus or Photoshopped hoaxes like this picture—because they felt like keys to a lock that no longer kept us safe.

An awkward moment passed as we sat quietly, trying to figure out what to say next.

I spoke first:

"Jesus," I said, shaking my head. "I mean, nobody's tried to . . ." I struggled to find the words.

He seemed to understand because he said, "People look different at me." He continued: "I have been asked three times to get the fuck out of your country," pointing at me on the stress of *your*. I'd never thought of it as mine and felt ashamed, then defensive. He shook his head, trying to smile but only managed a weak grimace.

"Idiots," I said, wanting to say something more but could only add, "Morons."

We started sipping our second beers, quickly at first when the silence seemed it might be short, and then slowly when we realized it wasn't. Pints in hand, we looked at the view as the lights finally came on. The beads of condensation from his other glass pooled and had begun to soak the picture, the different colored inks bleeding together.

"Anani sikeyim," I said finally, shaking my head. It was the only Turkish phrase I remembered. It meant motherfucker. Barish started laughing. He had taught it to me and he would always get a kick whenever I said it. I'd said it so much that year that it became part of my regular vocabulary, yelling it in the car whenever someone cut me off or when I was angry with my girlfriend about something.

When he'd first taught me the expression he said, "It means, 'I fuck your mother,'" pointing first at himself and then at me.

He laughed now, saying it too, nodding excitedly.

I was feeling better. The beer brought an ease over my body and I stood up, repeating the words again.

"Anani sikeyim," he echoed.

Then I said it again, louder, and again he answered. Something came over us. We fell into a loop and kept going, a little louder each time in between laughs, a bizarre call and response. He stood up and we moved over to the railing of the deck that looked out on downtown. "Anani sikeyim!" we yelled together, hands cupping our mouths. I watched all the cars driving away as memories from the previous year flooded my brain: the time Barish took me to a friend's house and we got high smoking a hookah; answering phone calls from his mother, who could only say "Hello," and trying to tell her that Barish wasn't home before I eventually just hung up; the night of my twenty-first when he took me out drinking and had to sneak me back into the dorm over his shoulder like a wounded war buddy.

We'd lose touch with one another for a long time after that night on the deck, but then, out of the blue, almost ten years later, I received an e-mail.

Unbelievable, I thought, looking at my inbox. I waited a few minutes, just staring at the subject line—Remember Me?—before I opened it. It made me nervous for some reason. Eventually I clicked on it. I could hear his voice in my head as I read over his words, catching me up on what he'd been doing the last few years, apologizing for not writing sooner. Buried in the last paragraph was the purpose of his e-mail: Barish was getting married and he was asking me to attend. Surprised by the invite, I was considering the expense of a plane ticket to Turkey when I realized that he was getting married here in the States. In all those years since I'd last seen him I thought of him only now and again, certain he'd moved back home. But here Barish was, like me, in Kansas City, inviting lost American friends to his wedding. It made me pity him, but I shouldn't have felt that way; it was a kindness to invite me back into his life. I wrote back, saying I wouldn't miss it for the world, then erased it and typed *I'd be honored to come*.

When I mentioned it to my wife, she said, "Who's Barish?"

"John," I said. "From college."

Still she looked confused.

"My roommate junior year."

"Your roommate . . ." she searched.

"The Turk," I said, confounded.

"Oh, the snorer," she said. "The Turk, sure."

"The snorer," I said, and fastened a printed copy of his e-mail with the details of time and place to the fridge with a magnet.

I didn't get to talk to Barish—he was using his birth name again—until after the ceremony and reception had finished. It was late in the night and most of the other guests had left. He and his pretty wife had a plane to catch early the next morning, but we stayed up late, along with a few other stragglers, an odd assortment of drunken uncles and cousins, catching up, drinking from a clear bottle of liquor I couldn't pronounce, strong enough to blind. How amazing to see him again, both of us grown men and married. We got drunk, told the old stories for our wives, and smiled over the vast stretches of silence, before he excused himself and his wife, so tired she could barely keep her eyes open. He picked her up, her dark arms curling listlessly around his neck, as he carried her to the limo. I watched them leave and wondered if we'd get together when he returned, just the two of us, as we promised. *Probably not*, I thought, trying to catch a glimpse of them through the tinted windows before they passed out of sight. But that all came so much later, years after that night on the deck in Wichita when we were young, scared, and lonely, yelling *motherfucker* in Turkish at the town below us. That night our shouting and laughter had become harsh, strained, the words feeling necessarily expelled from our bodies because we couldn't contain them any longer. I remember feeling the burn building in my lungs, and we went on a few seconds more until soon, like a fading coughing spell, I could sense it was almost out of our systems. A few people on the street below stopped, craning their necks to look up at us like we were crazy, as though we might jump, but instead we gathered ourselves, turned our gaze toward one another as our breathing slowed, and said it one more time.

Two Back, 1973

Before he let it kill him, the barn saved his life.

They called it Two Back because it belonged to Robert "Two Back" Cannery, who was once caught in the Johnston's wheat field making the beast with two backs all by himself. "Drop your pecker and get back to work, Cannery. Only thing I'm paying you to thresh is the wheat," Mr. Johnston had said, who was the father of one of Cannery's friends. They were in high school then, just kids, and had been suffering through Shakespeare in sophomore English that semester, so the nickname seemed to just present itself, fitting as it was, being Cannery had been caught, quite literally, red-handed. It was the kind of nickname that stuck immediately, like cudded gum to shoe sole. Yes, from then on it was Two Back for Cannery.

Years later, Cannery came up with the idea for the barn over a game of cards. His friends, who themselves had farms and families now, were gathered around Cannery's kitchen table, thumbing the dog-eared corners of three-of-a-kinds and straight flushes. At the epicenter of the round maple table sat a 1.75 of bourbon and it was upon taking a few sniffs that Cannery stood abruptly, threw down his cards, and declared he was going to build a barn, something he'd been thinking about for some time but had never mentioned. The others were silent, looking at each other, maybe raising an eyebrow, wondering if the juice had already ruined Cannery for the evening. "Shut up and bet, Two Back,"

Will Frighton finally said. "Yeah, make your goddamn bet, Two Back," the others echoed. "I'm sitting on a winner here while you're running your dang mouth." Cannery looked at his cards and threw a couple of pennies into the pot. "I said, by God, I mean to raise a gol darn barn out there," he repeated, slamming one hand on the table and pointing the other one at the wall of the kitchen that divided the men from the rolling Flint Hills surrounding them in all directions. Perturbed by a second interruption, Frighton had to be stilled by the others as he wrangled for Cannery, who stared calmly back. They pulled on his shoulder till he took to his chair again. The men looked at Cannery's hand, still frozen in the air, undisturbed by the commotion, and then down at their cards, shaking their heads, raising an eyebrow or two. "Drunk hisself stupid is all," Bob Wilson whispered. Having known him all their lives they'd seen how Cannery was always coming up with far-away ideas that never amounted to squat. Besides, the men knew—everyone in town knew—bad luck followed him around like a haunt. Like the time he drove a plow clear through Mr. Wilkerson's barn, having lost himself in the movement of the cloud patterns overhead. Like the way his fields always yielded less than everyone else's. Like how his wife couldn't bear children on account of his dead seed.

No one said anything about it and Cannery eventually sat down to flip over a small pair, losing for the third straight hand. But by the time Bob Wilson returned from his rusted old Ford with a second bottle—"thought we could use a extra"—the mood lightened and their smiles came easier. "Good thinking, Wilson," they hooted and clapped while upstairs Cannery's wife, Trudy, rolled over in bed, pulling the worn cotton sheets to her chin, the cool underside of the pillow over her ear. It was going to be a long night. So when Cannery said it again a couple hours later, down three dollars, Will Frighton's reprimand to "Shut up and bet your ass-sorry cards" was met with Don McCarthy's response: "Shut up yourself, Frighton. Worse than a sour old whore tonight. The man said he wants to build a barn, tired of throwing tarps and gunnysacks over all his equipment. Lord only knows that's understandable, ain't it? Hell, we should help him." Everyone at the table, all seven, nodded their heads with the ease the liquor loosed upon their bodies. And so it was settled that night on the breath of their whiskey oaths: they would help Cannery build his barn.

This was in the spring of 1958, when the men were readying to range burn, which was how they prepared for the sowing season. It meant burning the topsoil of their fields to cleanse the area and enrich the soil for replanting. That early spring, with a chill still in the air, the horizon would be alive with the intermittent fires from neighboring farms, and if one were stranger to the Flint Hills he might think he'd come upon the end of the world. All evening and night they'd burn, the men staying alert to ensure the fire didn't spread beyond control, and in the morning the charcoal clouds still lingered in the air and the smell carried from home to home as the collective ash scattered in the breeze and settled into the soil. But by early fall the men were unsettled to find that the usually abundant harvest in southeast Kansas had been all but reduced to nothing by an ungiving soil. The rainy season had ended earlier than usual with the sky allowing only the occasional drip. The dry summer and the deep-crusted strata of blanketing snow from the previous winter left corn and wheat yields pitifully low, reducing corn harvests from 150 bushels an acre to a paltry 25 or 30. The government was promising help, but the government was always promising help, so what the hell else was new? If that weren't bad enough, the warming weather sped up the pests' breeding cycles and expanded their range, increasing the chances of over-winter survival. There were rumors of plague. Weekly, Pastor Bryan sermoned on His judgment and everyone in town, congregated on the splintering pews of the dilapidated chapel, nodded their heads up and down. The men grew desperate, resorting to selling their emaciated livestock (as their great-grandfathers had done during the grasshopper invasion of 1874) and later their daughters' ponies to stay afloat. They hardly left their homes and for sometime no one mentioned Cannery's barn, barely even spoke to him at all for fear his ill fortune had brought this on the town. With all the lost time in the fields, the men began drinking through entire days, watching the sun rise and fall from their sunken porches.

It wasn't until some weeks later, with winter nearing, that Don Mc-Carthy came by Cannery's and things began to change. "Well ain't much else can go wronger. Show me what you're thinking," McCarthy said when he found Cannery scrawling in charcoal on a tablet of white paper, sketches of his barn. In addition to the general air of haplessness about him, Cannery's friends teased him for the interest he'd always taken in drawing. He'd been the one from the group to sketch passing fancies during class, daydreaming, or to stare off at sunsets during peak harvesting, losing precious hours of light. They couldn't understand why he wasted his time in such idle foolishness. But McCarthy wasn't chiding him now, rubbing his chin as he examined Cannery's plans. At the next game of cards, their first since the drought, with the men reduced to betting matchsticks, they resolved to begin work on Cannery's barn. Wasn't much else to do with things the way they were, they said. Cannery thought their pledges kind but wasn't expecting them to actually show, so when he saw Frighton and the others through the kitchen window the following morning, just able to make them out—ghostly figures, the whole lot of them—as they trudged through the early dawn towards his house, tools in hand, pulling carts of lumber, he was surprised, running to grab his tablet from the bureau. "What do they want, Robert?" Trudy said, over her shoulder, cracking an egg into the black skillet. Cannery brushed past her through the salt and sizzle of the kitchen to the door. "They're here to help with the barn." Trudy watched the white of her egg brown, the yolk harden, thinking, *the barn?*

They worked on the shortening cycle of daylight for the next few months through late fall and winter, during the hours they'd normally have been tending their own farms. The man from the bank in Wichita had said, "Are you sure you want to do this now, with the way things have been? Personally, I don't think it wise." But Cannery just smiled the way he always had in face of long odds, undaunted and confident, quickly signing his name on the loan.

It was in the early spring, with the thawing of the pestilent earth, that the men neared completion. They worked long days and soon developed a small crowd of spectators after the winter's passing, sometimes men and passersby, but mostly women and children coming to watch—some of them pleading for their husbands to come home for a change, while others came for the escape of having something to do. They'd really thrown themselves into it alright—these men who seemed to have given their lives over to slothfulness the past year, relying largely on their wives and field hands to run their families and farms. Trudy would bring pitchers of cool water and the occasional honeyed biscuit to offer in commiseration. And on the day when they finished in early April, after having added a second coat of red and painted the last of the white trim, people from all over town came to see the fruit of the men's labor. And they, Cannery and his friends, were proud. Here they had done something, worked hard, as when they were young. The red wooden beauty grew out of the ground where nothing had been before, taller than anyone else's for miles. A sight, for sure.

Cannery decided on a celebration, a dance the whole town would attend, folks coming from all over the Flint Hills. He decked the barn out as fancy as anything the Legion hall had ever seen and brought in fiddlers that made the saltiest soul tap his foot. Whiskey, cards, dancing. Everyone seemed to enjoy himself. Cannery was pleased, having finally seen something through without mishap. The looks he got from people were different now, less sorrowful and pitying than a validation, respectful. He always thought he'd give the barn a distinctive name—something from a fancy book—but before he had a chance to say otherwise it quickly developed his own, Two Back.

That ensuing year the earth gave back what it had withheld previously, bountifully. The men returned to tending their own farms but journeyed to Cannery's weekly to play cards in a little area of the barn away from the machinery and crop bins that Cannery left bare for such occasions, excepting a long oak table and the bottles of bourbon, of course. It was one such evening when Pastor Bryan showed up, knocking hard on those unweathered red slats, though the sound hardly made more than a hiccup inside the cavernous barn. He was coughing and Cannery motioned him inside. "Come on in here," Ed Wilson said.

They watched Pastor Bryan move cautiously inside. He looked shook up, sick maybe. Will Frighton extended his glass of bourbon but the pastor waved it off. "What's a matter, P.B.?" McCarthy said. They were all churchgoers, but truth be told they weren't the godliest of men, often sleeping through Pastor Bryan's sermonizing. Older than their young pastor, the men had taken to calling him "P.B." for short, kindly letting him know he wasn't above them just because he wore that collar and could speak of momentous matters. "The church is in trouble," the pastor said, shivering. "It's falling apart. Needs renovation, a new steeple." The men looked at each other, silent. Thinking he'd figured it out, Joe Johnston said, "You saw what we did with Two Back here and you want us to fix up your church." He was smiling. "Is that right?" The pastor shook his head and then looked at Cannery, who was unsettled by P.B.'s unyielding stare. Then he realized why the pastor had come and, after finally convincing the young man to sit down and have a drink for God's sake, that was the night Two Back became a church.

For the next three years Two Back housed Sunday's impassioned gatherings while funds were raised and the original church rebuilt, and souls traveled from miles around to sit on bales of hay and feel fear as Pastor Bryan spoke about God and man, animal and mineral. Collection hats circulated with S.O.S.: *Save Our Steeple* written in felt-tip pen across the side. It was back underneath the tarpaulin covers for Cannery's equipment, but he didn't much mind, for seeing the way people flooded through the doors of his barn, complimenting him so pleasantly, filled him with a sense of genuine satisfaction he realized long missing. When service let out, Cannery would stand outside the large red and white doors, a few feet behind Pastor Bryan, shaking hands with the folks who were filing out of Two Back, returning their smiles and touch. "See you folks next Sunday. Come and receive the healing." And soon a strange thing happened, further validating Cannery and his barn: of their own accord people started referring to him as Robert again, and when they spoke the words Two Back they were referring only to the barn. Cannery came to love Sundays, nearly as much as the

nights he and his pals played cards. So when those three years passed
and it came time for the church to move to its newly fashioned home,
Cannery saddened, moping around Two Back alone, kicking dirt. He
didn't want things to change, had unspokenly hoped Pastor Bryan
would permanently settle the congregation there, seeing how much
folks seemed to like it so. When he confronted Pastor Bryan about it,
the mealy-mouthed young man had thanked him for his service, and,
when Cannery persisted, lowered his voice, saying, "There is a war going on, Robert. People need comfort—they need guidance. And God,
well, God needs a real house of worship, not a barn." The ingratitude
of which filled Cannery with a dyspeptic rancor. He stopped attend-
ing church altogether, instead watching from the upstairs window as
Trudy slid into the old Ford—"I have to go," she said resolutely—to
drive the three miles to church, where she would sit alone in the hard-
backed pew, offering excuses and apologies for Cannery's absence.

It was about the time when people in town were learning to distin-
guish Vietnamese from Vietcong that Cannery came up with an idea
that would return people to Two Back. He'd read about it in a maga-
zine near the train depot in Wichita, and so moved by the possibility
he decided to try his hand running picture shows inside the barn. He
spoke to a man in Kansas City who ran three movie houses and the
man had tried to discourage Cannery from the idea. "Movies is a bad
idea right now. Don't you know there's a war out there that people get
to watch free of charge every night on their television sets?" But when
Cannery proved his commitment unwavering, the man began speaking
dizzyingly of things like start-up capital, demographics, and markets,
a wild-eyed craze to his tone, and he agreed to talk to his distributor
about the "rural draw" of pictures being untapped. But such possibility
came not without sacrifice, and to get the money needed to start Cannery had to give up farming, consenting to sell off his plow and tractor,
nearly all his acreage, leaving only the house and the barn for himself.
It was a gamble, but what wasn't? he explained to Trudy, who, just-in-
formed, let her chin fall to her chest, puffing out folds of skin from her

neck. His friends thought he was crazy. "Why the hell'd you go and do that for?" they said when he started out with the second-run pictures, thinking Cannery had been swindled by the fast-talking city man. But folks around there didn't much care how old the films were; they were just pleased not to have to drive clear out to Wichita.

And the people did come back, as Cannery had hoped. It was just as he envisioned it: folks traveled from as far as three towns over and paid to sit in Two Back, on the same bales of hay that had cushioned the hams of churchgoers before them. He started out showing movies on Saturdays only but really turned a profit when he began showing them on Wednesdays and Fridays as well, selling the place clean out and breaking even in only three years. A few months later, as a little blasphemous screw-you to P.B. he began showing Sunday matinees, stealing nearly half of the church's draw. Cannery would take tickets at the door with Trudy selling cups of cold cola and lemonade at a nickel apiece. When it was time for the show to start, Cannery would welcome his guests and ceremonially unfurl the large white sheet comprised of six linens Trudy had stitched together, and then climb up the ladder to the hay-covered loft to work the projector, as the man from Kansas City had shown him. From there, once the reel was set, Cannery looked down at all the folks below him, the couples holding hands or furtively touching one another, the children who came to every show, the one or two families who had never been to a movie before. When the projector rumbled to life, the bright light shot over their heads in a straight powerful line to the white sheet. And with the movie starting, the bright colors that flamed against their still bodies filled Cannery with the same awe that caused him to stop and stare at the sky or pick up charcoal to sketch.

For several years it was this way, but then, with the certainty that many in town had quietly asserted, Cannery's ill fortune returned in the tornado season of '73, which laid waste to much of southeastern Kansas. Cannery had turned off the radio, but sensed the twister's approach in the ominously green, dead air. Soon the hail came, falling like stones from an angry God. It took all of Trudy's strength and pleading to get him to leave the barn and follow her to the cellar, and there Cannery sat on an upturned crate, while Trudy huddled at his side, and they listened as it tore the barn apart, slats, shingles, and siding racketing off their house. In the morning, with the break of light, Cannery ventured out to collect the disparate pieces of Two Back, spread as far in the distance as he could see, stooping to drag the scattered limbs back to his house. He picked up the weathervane and held the hard metal in his hand. The pit in his stomach grew as he gathered what he could. "We should be thankful, Robert," Trudy said, following him. With a godly fickleness, the tornado had settled down on the barn and quickly risen to the sky again, as these storms were wont to do, not touching down for another quarter mile. He looked back at his untouched house. "We should be thankful," Trudy whispered.

Some weeks later, on an afternoon when Trudy was gone to church, Cannery went to play cards at Joe Johnston's, where the game had been moved after the tornado took Two Back. The entire time Cannery sat silently listening to the others painfully take care to avoid speaking of Two Back, talking about damn near everything else: the upcoming planting season, the hot weather, their plans for range-burning soon. Johnston's son, just back from the war, sat quietly in the corner of the room holding a glass of water. He was pale and thin, still dressed in full uniform, and whenever someone spoke to him he'd look away and fill his glass from a water pitcher at his feet. Cannery failed to discern his name from the rest of Johnston's brood, recalling only his face—that of a young boy's, clinging to Johnston's legs as he tried to walk. "Must've been hell to come home to this," Cannery said. It was the first voluntary thing he'd uttered all night, and the men shut up, looking at Cannery and then Johnston's son, but he just leaned forward, picking up the pitcher, and filled his glass a sip's worth. Cannery had meant it must have been hell to come back home to a tornado but realized the implications and ambiguity of this.

"Wore out is all he is," Johnston said, then slapped Cannery on the arm. "Now let's see what your cards say." Cannery flipped them over, a loser. He won not a single hand and after an hour or so quietly stood and walked to the door. The others watched him return home through the window, exhaling a collective "Sssshhhhiiiittt."

It was a short time later, a day or so maybe, as he sat on his porch drinking Millers from a blue cooler at his feet, that he saw a young man approaching in the distance. It was his first visitor since the insurance inspector had visited in person to inform Cannery his plan had covered fire and flood, not tornado. Cannery blinked a few times now to make sure he hadn't nodded off, being that he barely slept anymore. He lay in bed most nights listening to Trudy soughing laboriously in her sleep until he got up and walked around outside in the thick night air.

This man was wearing a military uniform with bright patches and medals, colorful ribbons bundled together in a neat square of his chest like a tract of variously cropped land. He looked like he could have been Johnston's son, though now he seemed even thinner, paler, more gaunt. He nodded at Cannery. "Just got back," he said in a strange and broken country manner, adding "from the war" when Cannery said nothing. He barely opened his mouth when he spoke, as though it pained him to do so, perhaps injured. Cannery looked at where the soldier's name was on the uniform but couldn't make it out, bad vision and all. "You Johnston's boy?" he asked, but the soldier just looked down, kicking languidly at some dirt. "I use to come here before I left," the soldier said, meeting Cannery's silent stare directly. "I'd brung my girl and we'd watch your shows. Your pictures. She use to let me touch her, there in the dark," he said, smiling a private smile that made Cannery wish he were inside his head so he could see exactly what the soldier was remembering. Cannery thought of the nights after shows when he'd clean up, how he'd have to broom over the spilled soda cups and half-eaten apples, dust and lint streaming over the occasional stains of semen and blood. "When I was over there and things got hairy, all I thought of was sitting right there in the dark with Alice Anne, hoping she might let my hand slide inside her dress, but still liking the picture alright if she didn't." Cannery pointed out to where his barn used to stand and began to say something, but then stopped, lowered his arm and exhaled. "Look son, they got shows an hour and some minutes from here, out towards Wichita," he finally said, but the soldier shook his head. "I just mean to tell you what I come for." He looked out at the expanse and then back at Cannery. "She left me while I was gone." Cannery moved to speak but no words escaped his mouth. "Thought I might find her here when I got back in the world again, but I see you've had something stolen from you, too." The soldier looked out at where Two Back used to stand, whispering to himself, "Me, the war. You, the torn-ado." He said it again, this time quieter, and then he turned to leave. Cannery stooped to grab him a beer. "Hey," he said, calling the man back, feeling something move inside him for the first time in weeks. "Come back." He wanted to listen to the soldier talk, and so he did, all afternoon and into the evening, listening to his stories about war, though the soldier shook off Cannery's offers of drink.

"What you gonna do now?" the soldier asked sometime later, lifting his chin in the direction where the barn had stood. "Gonna build another?" Cannery considered this a minute, something he'd done often since the tornado. After paying off his initial loan on the barn and with no insurance money coming in, it wouldn't be long before he was near broke. There was the twice-mortgaged house and the square of land that he'd plowed under to make room for the barn. That was it. "No, movies is over for me," he finally said, feeling the whole venture had been misguided, led astray again by his whim. Then the idea, which came with the rush of realization, presented itself. "Started out a farmer, didn't I? Heck, that's what I'll be again. Still got a little land left," he said, cracking open another beer, "ain't much more than football field's worth but that's something. Nuff to live on, I spose." The more he spoke, the more Cannery found himself taking on the soldier's manner of speaking, aping his posture and gesticulations.

The idea so moved him that Cannery stood quickly and stumbled a little as he walked off the porch and around the side of the house, appearing a minute later with two drums of gasoline. "Come on off that porch and give me a hand, will you," he said to the soldier, who followed Cannery out to where the barn had been. The summer night was sweating, thick and sticky. Cannery tilted his drum so that gasoline began to spill out, walking slowly so that the viscous liquid left a trail behind. "You too," he said to the soldier, who started doing the same thing. "This here is called a range burn, son," he said into the air. The evening was turning into night all around him and soon Trudy arrived home after a long day of collecting donations and selling baked goods at the church. She looked at Cannery and wearily said, "What are you up to, possessed so?" He was hunched over a gasoline drum, mumbling to himself, and he looked up once just long enough to say range burn and wave her inside.

"Range burn," he continued, speaking over his shoulder to the soldier as he continued to spill gas onto the dusty earth below. "This," Cannery said as the last drops trickled from the drum, "is how we start again." He stopped, seeing that now he was standing where the hand-hewn walnut center post had stood, and felt the weariness deep inside his bones. Dark now, he could still trace the edges of large cloud masses in the black sky overhead. He closed his eyes and the memories were upon him again. Farming, the church, picture shows. All those years seemed to converge within him at that moment and he felt nowhere and everywhere.

When he opened his eyes, he couldn't see the soldier. He looked around, saw the empty drum sitting alone, and in the distance thought maybe he could just make out a lone figure pass over a hillock, disappearing into the darkened horizon. Striking a match off his belt, he lit a few pieces of wood that had been part of Two Back and threw them to the ground. The fire caught rapidly, shooting all around him on the dribbled path of damp soil Cannery and the soldier had traveled with the gasoline. He stepped away from the flames. Being so close made the sound of catching fire deafening, but there outside it was silent for miles and miles around him. Out there people were sleeping in their beds, dreaming the same old terrors from childhood or turning up the volume on their new color televisions to watch repeated footage of helicopters carrying the last soldiers from Saigon, civilians clinging to the runners in hopes of being taken away.

Exhausted, Trudy went upstairs and crawled into bed. She tried to stay awake until Cannery came to join her but was already snoring in a matter of minutes, a wearisome and angry kind of sleep. Then, awoken by the sound—like an endless line of wet clothes snapping in a gusty wind—and light reflecting off the mirrors of her bedroom, Trudy crept to the window and peaked through the inch between curtain and sill. From there she watched as Cannery looked around one last time and walked into the fire. Her mouth opened but nothing came out and she turned away, quickly slipping back into bed, where she pulled the covers to her neck, pausing there as she shut her eyes, then continued, stretching the sheets up and over her head.

Birthday

THERE WAS A RHYTHM TO IT, the starting and stopping, and despite the fact that there were no other cars on the road, Alan came to full and complete rests at every intersection. He was driving west, up side streets on the periphery of Lawrence Memorial Hospital, having to pause every hundred feet or so of the grid at a stop sign. He thought this would be a quicker route to the highway, but, in his exhaustion, had failed to realize that at 2 a.m. the main roads wouldn't have been crowded. The lulling quality of this cycle betrayed the urgency he was supposed to be feeling, and he slipped so far inside his own thoughts that he disconnected from the actions his body performed: hands on the steering wheel, guiding but not directing; eyes on the road, open but not seeing. Driving but not driving.

He was headed to the medical center in Kansas City, and somewhere in the air above him inside a yellow helicopter was his newborn son, spending last breaths from his failing lungs.

He had thought he might be able to follow the helicopter as he drove, but he couldn't find it now. It was an absurd notion, he knew, but Alan couldn't help the way his eyes strayed toward the sky every few minutes, thinking somehow it might appear and he could simply follow, like a funeral train behind police escort. But as he looked at the sky now there was only the dark expanse of a starless night. He readjusted his grip on the wheel, knuckles flaring white against the brown leather, and felt the encroaching weariness of a long day finally catching up with him.

It had started out, as all Tuesdays were, a normal day in clinic. He was an ophthalmologist and had a small practice in Lawrence, north of the river. Between patients his assistant Sharon slipped him a note that said his wife needed to talk to him immediately. She had paged him twice already, but he was running thirty minutes behind schedule and Mr. Greenleaf, a curmudgeonly old man who had long-suffering cataracts and a quick temper, was waiting; his patients, Alan believed, deserved his full attention. After looking into the milky sockets for the fourth time in as many months Alan again told Greenleaf he needed surgery, and as he'd done the other three appointments the old man guffawed and said, "Isn't there something you could just prescribe?" Alan told him that what he prescribed was surgery, and Greenleaf looked away, huffing, and then mumbled under his breath, finally saying he would need to think about it. They agreed on a four-week follow up. As Alan walked him to the front desk to check out, Greenleaf confided that it was his daughter who made him keep coming back. "She wants me to have the surgery—won't let up on me," he shrugged. "Says I'll go blind otherwise. But the way I see it there ain't much worth looking at no how." The comment made Alan stop walking. It goaded him that people like Greenleaf, whose illnesses could be remedied, wouldn't accept help. Alan tried to smile, saying he agreed with Greenleaf's daughter, and then offered the elderly man a firm handshake. He checked two boxes on the billing sheet—shaking his head, *Why wouldn't he have the surgery?*—and handed it to the girl at the front desk, then calmly walked back to his office, shut the door, and called home.

Sue picked up, a frantic timbre to her voice—"Something's wrong." He tried to keep her calm, intoning softly for her to tell him what had happened. She was always getting worked up over things, but this was partly why their relationship worked, Alan reasoned; they balanced one another, their temperaments the yin and yang of excitability. "I think I'm—it's too early," was what she said. She was late in her seventh month. He told her sometimes that happened and it wasn't out of the ordinary. "Alan, I'm bleeding," she interrupted. He felt the uncomfortable prickling of surprise but remained poised, exhaling and keeping the same steady tone he used when patients came in with ghastly eye injuries, bloody retinas and crushed sockets. He asked her how much. "I've got a bath towel between my legs and it's completely soaked." His finger that had been flicking his computer mouse back and forth stopped. He looked at the screen and then at the wall where his diplomas hung neatly in chronological order. It was happening. She was in trouble. For a moment there was only Sue's breathing, stirring in his ear. Then she said his name.

"Call an ambulance. Now," he said, standing up and easing his chair out with the backs of his knees. She'd already called for one, she said.

"I was trying to get a hold but couldn't wait any longer."

He felt the cool plastic of the phone against his lip. "I'll meet you at the hospital," he said, forcing his voice to steady, and then rushed out of his office, telling Sharon to reschedule everyone; his wife was in labor.

Alan looked at the clock on his dash, 2:13 a.m., as he pulled away from the last stop sign and collected a ticket at the toll before finally veering onto I-70. He was forty minutes away from the medical center, thirty-five if he really sped. He settled on eight miles over the limit as a safe transgression; he would be delayed even longer if pulled over, he reasoned. His view of the sky opened up now that he was on the highway, and he scanned the horizon once more, looking for the faintest sign of the helicopter—multicolored lights perhaps—and listened for the whirring of blades, spinning the child away into the early morning. There was nothing, though, just the periodic strobe of radio towers beating against the pall and the sound of his air conditioner filling the car with a staticky un-noise.

The first few hours of labor had flown by in the bustle and commotion of Sue's arrival at the hospital, but as she stabilized time seemed to slow and the night wore on. Despite being premature and despite the loss of blood, it appeared that everything was progressing quite well, all things considered. Alan had held his wife's hand as the contractions grew closer and closer, feeling in her grip the longing and desire for the child she'd talked about since before they married almost seven years ago, and that desire seemed stronger than anything he might ever know himself. This had become the burden on their otherwise contented marriage. Sue wanted a big family, several children at least, but it didn't come easy for her, pregnancy. Three times already, after long struggles to conceive, her body failed to carry to term, and now the expectations for that big family had diminished to the insistent struggle for a single child.

Though he'd never have admitted it to Sue, the miscarriages hadn't upset Alan. Well, no, they had—they upset him greatly, in fact, less for the lost child, however, than for the toll they took on Sue. Thrice she'd been devastated and each time he'd tried to console her while secretly harboring his shame for feeling some amount, however small, of relief. The truth was he never wanted to be a father. What he wanted was Sue and, for her happiness, this was a concession he was willing to make. He'd never warmed to idea of being a father, partly because his relationship with his own had been difficult, but more than that, he supposed when confronting his baser desires, he was selfish. While his friends were dutifully having children they'd have to restructure their lives around, Alan found himself on the outskirts of forty feeling free and content. He'd grown to like his life as it was, the two of them, he and Sue: they had a nice home they'd restored in Old West Lawrence; his practice, while small, was continuing to grow steadily—he was looking to take on a partner in the next year. Things were comfortable. But he worried that for Sue this would never be enough, and time was running out. Sue was thirty-nine, two years older than Alan, and with each passing birthday, for every year after her thirty-fourth, she'd talked about the increased difficulty of conceiving or cited some new statistic about the risks of children being born with birth defects. When she'd say this, Alan would hold her and then they'd sit down and go through the tiresome process of developing a schedule for having intercourse at the most opportune times of the month, which had turned their sex life into a utilitarian formula of cycles and appointments, something Alan detested. But he went along with it, and they would try, and yet with each miscarriage he'd seen Sue grow a little quieter, her spirit seeming to diminish a little more. After the last time, nearly a year and a half ago, she sat in the large white chair in their bedroom and cried until she couldn't anymore and then rocked back and forth, knees to chest, for nearly a week as he brought her food that she picked at and finally ignored.

One such evening, struggling for conversation as they forked through salads, Alan casually mentioned that a friend of his from med school had adopted a little boy. Sue, wearing the same gray sweatpants and sweatshirt that she had all week, stabbed a grape tomato and raised it to her mouth, holding it there before her lips. "Good for him," she said, and with the decisiveness of a judge lowering her gavel she forced the tomato into her mouth, and adoption was never again discussed as anything other than an excellent option for other people.

Weeks later, when she'd started to come out of it, Sue asked Alan to touch her body again. Afterwards, in the midnight stillness that followed making love, Sue said that it was unfair that they hadn't been able to bear the fruit of their intimacy. Alan listened, coming down from the high of climax, and silently stroked his wife's back as she leaned into his chest. He lay there, thinking that, while unfair, it was also completely natural. Unfortunate, yes, but natural in a world where people were born blind or deformed and others had genes that would never let them see a day past fifty. This was biology and it had nothing to do with fairness. "It'll happen," he said as his fingertips crept up her nape to the roots of her hair.

"Maybe not," she said, looking up into his eyes, her fingertips moving slowly across his chest.

"I think it'll happen," he said, pausing a moment after seeing the change his irresolute consolation brought to her eyes, and then he pulled her closer and affirmed, "We'll have a child, I'm certain."

It was dark in the room. Sue seemed like she might have smiled and leaned forward to kiss him, saying she loved him, before rolling over and pulling his arm around her, close to her chest. As he'd done many times before, he said what she needed to hear, though it made him uncomfortable; he would never honestly be able give her certainty. And then, as she often did before drifting to sleep, she asked Alan to tell her what their child would be like and he whispered softly to her until she slipped into to dream, tussling a little and moving her back flush against him. He felt the push of her skin against his and finally closed his eyes. There in the dark, listening to her breathe, he faced the tough realization that though she meant everything to him, he alone would never be enough to keep her happy.

Earlier that evening at the hospital, though, it seemed their luck had changed, and for the first time there was a real chance. Despite being premature, things were stable, Dr. McQuillan said. Alan had arrived as they were prepping Sue and McQuillan came over, slapped him on the shoulder, and said, "Ready to be a daddy?" Alan told him to take care of her, that she'd lost a lot of blood. McQuillan nodded his head slowly up and down, as though maybe in exaggeration or annoyance, and said not to worry, that things were under control, as he slapped Alan on the shoulder again. He was a large, overweight man and was known for cursing at his nurses or throwing the occasional tantrum while he worked. But he was the best around, everyone assured Alan. And there in the delivery room McQuillan did seem to have things under control. While noisome otherwise, under these circumstances his strong, confident personality comforted Alan.

But suddenly things had changed later, and prior to the birth, in the space of what seemed only thirty seconds, his son's heart rate dropped to almost nothing. *The child is in grave danger*, Alan thought when he heard McQuillan tell his nurse that he would need an anesthesiologist immediately. Alan stood beside the bed, holding his wife's hand, feeling helpless against the chaos that had so quickly crept into the room. There were more people now, another doctor and several nurses scurrying around, speaking in the quick, terse argot of emergency.

One of the nurses urged Alan away from Sue's side, saying he could stay in the room but had to move away from the bed. "I'm staying right here," he said, squeezing Sue's hand. The nurse looked at a loss and before mustering a response a much deeper voice sounded from behind them:

"No time to be a goddamn hero, Alan. Get the hell away from there." Alan turned to see McQuillan in his oversized scrubs looking down at him with his small, gray eyes. "This is serious. You should know better than anyone here," his voice filtered through the blue mask. Inside, Alan felt his warring selves tangle, doctor and husband. He stood up and faced McQuillan. Alan didn't want to leave Sue's side, but he realized McQuillan was right. He would be helping more by allowing everyone to do their jobs and staying out of the way, so he rose, letting her hand go, and stepped away.

"I'll be right there," he said, pointing to the wall on the opposite side of the room, but Sue was crying, asking what was happening, eyes darting all over the room. Her brown hair was stringy with sweat, matted to her flushed cheeks. "It's okay, sweetheart," Alan said a little louder. "Everything's fine. You're doing wonderful." He moved back against the wall and watched the nurses set up a curtain over his wife's chest, visually dividing both mother from child and Alan from his wife. They were preparing her for a C-section. Alan felt a delayed rush of anger pass through him as he looked at McQuillan, wanting to push him away from Sue and take care of her himself, but as a doctor he was useless; his expertise never moved below the cheekbone. He'd delivered a few babies as a young resident in Seattle, thrown to the wolves on the graveyard E.R. shift, but that seemed ages ago, and his skill was so acutely localized in one area now that watching an obstetrician work made him feel like a deep right fielder trying to pick up the nuances of a slider.

The baby's pulse moved slowly across the EKG in small waves. Standing against the wall, he could see all the blood she'd lost, her gown damp in spots. Though the nurse had toweled most of it away, there was the faint residue, dried and cracking, on her thighs. "Where is this fucker?" McQuillan said over his shoulder to his nurse. "Didn't you page him?" The nurse scurried away. McQuillan sat on a stool, an unsettling calm having come over him, looking around the room as though at any second he might rise and say *Okay, Alan, I've gotten you this far—now you're on your own* and walk away. But just as quickly McQuillan snapped out of it, shooting off the chair and saying he couldn't wait any longer for the anesthesiologist to arrive. "We'll have to open her up under straight local," he said. Alan knew great pain was about to be inflicted on his wife. Her tumescent belly sat before McQuillan's peppery head, and quickly without pause, to Alan's surprise, he began to cut. Sue's initial groans and exhalations, quick and deep like they'd been earlier that day on the phone, gave way to screams.

Alan started to yell her name before catching himself. She cried again. "I'm right here," he called to her. He pushed off from the wall and took a few steps forward, but felt a hand latch on to his arm. Alan turned around to face a stubbly-chinned guy with mussed hair, clearly woken from sleep. His scrubs were only half on.

"I think we better stay right here," the guy said. The anesthesiologist. He was just a kid though. He'd finally shown up, minutes late. "Come on," he said, letting go of Alan's arm and motioning with his head towards the wall. Sue cried out again, and Alan turned quickly to the anesthesiologist. He wanted to throw all his weight into shoving the him against the wall, but let it pass when Sue cried out again. "She's going to be fine," the kid said, calm. "Dr. McQuillan has everything under control."

Alan shook his head, exhaling once, hard through his nostrils, and, as he often did when moved to anger, fell silent, packing it all in. He looked at McQuillan's head looming over Sue's stomach and found himself turning away with each incision. Years of surgery, malady, and disease had hardened any sort of aversion to blood and flesh but this was different. *Sue*, he thought, again standing on his tiptoes, trying to see her face. But a few seconds later, as the soles of Alan's shoes were hitting the floor, McQuillan was already pulling the baby out, saying something Alan couldn't hear. He handed the child to a blanket-towing nurse who enveloped the baby boy and whisked him away to another room.

"See," the anesthesiologist said. "Congratulations, buddy," he said, slapping his hand hard against Alan's doughy bicep before turning to leave.

As Alan started moving towards Sue, McQuillan stepped in front of him, holding up the palms of his blood-covered gloves for Alan to stop. Alan looked at them as McQuillan informed him they would need to medevac the child to KU Med in Kansas City, where there was a newborn intensive care unit. The fair skin above McQuillan's mask was blotchy and mottled, slick with sweat.

"But how is he, Ed?" Alan asked.

McQuillan looked over at the doctor who'd spelled him, sewing up Sue's stomach, and turned back: "Critical." Then he pulled the blue mask below his chin and wiped at his wet face with a towel. His look softened. Alan wondered if this was how he appeared to the family members of his own patients. He'd never been in this role before as husband, only as a son, years ago when his father had taken ill. "She's lost a lot of blood, Alan. We've got to keep her here at least for tonight." McQuillan turned away and a nurse removed the curtain. Alan met eyes with Sue. He moved to her side and reached for her hand. She was disoriented, drugged and crying.

"Where is he?" she kept saying. "Where is my son?"

"He's okay, honey," Alan said, rubbing her hand. "He's just early and they need to take him to Kansas City—to the med center." Her eyes began darting around the room again, looking all over, her chin tremulous. "They have the best care for newborns."

"Is he going to be okay?" she insisted. Alan opened his mouth but couldn't say anything. He looked down, touching a bead of sweat on her arm, and she began to cry. He pushed the sweat around in a circle, and when he looked up, she was staring him straight in the eye.

"You have to go," she said, the urgency clouding her face. "Now," she said, pushing him away from her. "Leave." Alan didn't want to go; she was in danger, too. He wanted to stay right where he was, but she was insistent, and so he turned away from her and left. "Go!"

. . .

Outside of Leavenworth Alan paid the toll, leaving only a short stretch of highway ahead of him before arriving in the city. As he adjusted the settings on his dash, he wondered if the helicopter was already at the hospital. Surely. He wasn't that far away himself now. He had been to the medical center many times, visiting sick friends and patients he'd transferred to doctors who worked out of the area. It wasn't far from the house where Alan grew up, from where his mother still lived. The major hospital in the city, it was where his father had stayed at the end. He'd died shortly before Alan and Sue met. Prostate cancer, a disease that ran amongst the men of his family the way hair loss does in most. His grandfather, two uncles, and his father had all died of it.

It was the same thing that would kill Alan.

As a doctor, he knew that no matter how well he took care of himself there were some things that were genetically determined. It didn't matter if he worked out, ate well, scheduled regular appointments and checkups; his fate always hung before him, ominously bright and clear, like a full moon.

Soon after finding out it was terminal, his father had augured over a phone call that he was going to live through Thanksgiving, Christmas, and his wife's birthday in January, still several months away. The doctors weren't giving him that long, but he'd made up his mind and that was that. Edna's birthday became the marker by which he'd allow himself to die. Alan was a resident in Seattle then. In subsequent calls Alan made between marathon shifts at the hospital, his father repeated his resolve, but no one actually expected him to make it to January, hoping he'd go before the pain became unbearable. It had been a tough time for Alan. He would finish a long shift in Seattle and then call his father in Kansas City and listen to him talk, so tired Alan could barely speak.

When his father had weathered the disease into December, Alan took personal leave for the holidays and returned home to Kansas City. He spent time with his father in his room at the medical center and watched him grow sicker and sicker, though the determination was still there in his eyes. His father was barely verbal by then, and Alan would sit quietly, the television talking for them. So many times he wanted to ask his father, *Why hang on?* He wanted to say everything would be fine; it was okay to die. With each passing holiday there was an equal sense of dread and relief, and when Edna's birthday came, his father was too sick to move so they brought the party to his room. He lay there in bed, a withering face amidst a heap of blankets, with Edna sitting in a chair beside him, trying to look as proud and happy as she could, maneuvering around the tubing to take hold of his hand. When Alan thought back on that sad time, his father's pained expression seemed to say *This will be you one day.* He lay in bed, a little closer to the end with each passing minute, watching Alan and the others as they ate cake and filled plastic flutes with champagne. Family members milled about, conversing softly, mustering smiles, talking Chiefs, and looking out the window at the falling snow as day passed into night. And sure enough, as he'd said, the next morning his father died.

There were times Alan felt cheated for knowing his fate, and at his lowest points he'd wondered what there was to live for if he was going to die early anyway. The answer was Sue, of course, the answer was helping people who needed care, but now it made him wonder if even the child were to survive, would it be fair to bring him into the world under an all but certain death sentence? In the car now he thought back to McQuillan pulling the child from Sue's stomach. For a brief instant he'd seen the boy, so small and blue, eyes closed and trembling, that Alan was sure he would never survive. He may not have delivered a baby in fifteen years but he remembered what the troubled ones looked like and suddenly he was ashamed that he and Sue had ever told anyone they were having a baby. He was imagining having to explain what happened—again they lost the child—to everyone at the office and then their friends and family. The hushed tones, *I'm so sorrys,* and cavernous hugs he wanted to disappear into. He thought of Sue, crushed, rocking in her chair. He thought of those nights in bed when she'd ask him to tell her what their child would be like. What could he possibly say to her now?

Which was worse, he thought: to father a child he couldn't fully love or to suffer its passing? Neither answer satisfied and contemplating the question made him ease off the accelerator, dropping far below the limit. He drove like this for a few minutes, thinking. And then he said it aloud to himself, the words leaping unexpectedly from his throat—the thought that till then was unutterable: he hoped the child was dead.

He was on the outskirts now, driving past the industrial ruins of the city, the empty warehouses, abandoned buildings, and barely functioning plants—skeletons animated only by the occasional passing train or graffiti artist tags. At three in the morning it was beautiful the way the dark horizon sparkled with the colored lights of the distant signs and buildings of downtown. In a few minutes he would see the rising shape of the medical center.

As Alan got off the highway, he took the curve of the exit ramp a little too fast and had to brake hard at the yield sign before moving onto the slower city streets. The car was new, a black Mercedes S-Class. He'd always driven Hondas but had indulged this whim after the decision to take on a partner. He was still getting used to its smooth handle. He was surprised to see the number of cars out so late. At a stoplight he closed his eyes, feeling the exhaustion, and leaned his head against the steering wheel. A few seconds later, with his eyes still shut, he was jolted by the sound of a horn. He opened his eyes and looked in the rearview where there was a car behind him. He could see a man behind the wheel with his hands palm up, his lips moving. The man honked again. Alan squinted into the rearview and for a moment he thought about throwing the car in park just to see what this jerk would do. The hospital though, he needed to keep going, and instead he put his right hand in the air and nodded as though to say I know, I know as his foot depressed the accelerator.

He drove down the street, through the rough neighborhoods that surrounded the medical center, and continued to watch the man, Alan's eyes lifting from the road to the rearview every few seconds. The man was tailgating, right on his bumper. What the hell was his problem? Alan thought about pulling over and letting him pass, but he didn't want to give him the satisfaction, continuing on in the direction of the med center. The man stayed behind Alan for a couple more blocks until they pulled behind another car, again stopped at a red light. Looking into the rearview, Alan tried to discern the man's features. He was black, wearing a red ball cap, so Alan couldn't see his eyes. He appeared younger than Alan, late twenties maybe, and, as if Alan had wronged him in some way, angry. The man was driving a new SUV that seemed out of place moving alongside the broken-down cars that limped through the area.

Alan's eyes moved from the rearview to the clock on his dash. He thought again of Sue. She'd be expecting to hear from him soon. He was tired but anxious, conscious of his pulse. Again he leaned his head forward to the steering wheel, eyes closed. He thought of Sue lying in her bed at the hospital. He imagined having to tell her the child didn't make it and hoping that when it passed, her tears and anger, she would somehow still be the same person he'd always loved, and more so, that she'd still love him. Suddenly he heard it again, the abrasive sound of the man laying into the horn. It startled Alan and he let his foot fall too fast on the pedal, sending his car into the bumper of the station wagon in front of him. Though he'd had hardly any momentum, Alan's head rocketed back into the headrest, on rebound from impact. He shook his head and looked at the car in front of him, a beat-up jalopy not worth the cost to insure it. Last thing he needed. For a moment he considered driving on. But what if someone were hurt? he thought, and put on his hazards.

As he opened his door the man in the SUV pulled alongside, looking as though he might stop, and then sped down the street. Alan stepped out of the car, running a few steps in that direction, shouting, "Thanks for stopping!" He kicked his heal against the broken pavement and quickly inspected his car—there wasn't much damage, a scuff that could be easily buffed out—before walking toward the station wagon. Though he didn't feel injured, he slowly rocked his head in circles as he neared the driver's-side door. Alan bent to the window. It was tinted and he could barely make out the form inside. He made a circle motion with his hand. "Are you alright?" Alan said, as the window began to lower manually. A white, haggard face appeared, tan and weathered, the face of a man who worked in the sun all day. He had long brown hair that fell to his chin. He looked like some of the hard-luck Medicaid patients Alan sometimes saw in clinic, whom he agreed to treat knowing he'd receive little back from the state. The man couldn't have been more than forty years old, but his face said he'd lived sixty. He was holding a hand at the back of his neck, rubbing in circles. "Are you okay?" Alan repeated. "Is anyone hurt?"

"Why'd you hit me?" the man said. His voice was high, squeaky almost, the pitch of one who enjoyed complaining. Not what Alan expected.

"I'm sorry. I . . . I didn't mean to. I was distracted and the person behind me—"

He'd lowered the window only a few inches and Alan could barely see inside. "You hit my car," the man said, slapping the steering wheel. "That ain't cool."

"No. I realize this," Alan said. He tried to look beyond the man, into his car, but the window was still mostly rolled up, a little smoke from a cigarette escaping. He could make out the trash in the footwell, a pile of upturned fast food cups. Alan was bending over with his hands on his knees.

"What the hell, man. Is there damage?"

Alan stood up. "I," he began, stretching out the word as he looked back at the blinking hazard lights of his own car, "don't know. Look, can we settle this later? I really have to go. My wife—there's been an emergency." He reached into his wallet for a card.

"I'll say you got yourself an emergency—you hit me, asshole!" The door sprang open, forcing Alan to back up a few feet, and the man slid out quickly, throwing it shut behind him. A small cloud of smoke billowed out after him. Alan could smell the marijuana hovering in the air between them. This guy had been so stoned he probably spaced off and didn't move when the light turned. Hell, most likely this wasn't even Alan's fault.

The man swiveled his shoulders back and forth, hands at his waist, grimacing a bit, and then stopped when he saw Alan was watching him. He was wearing faded blue jeans and a t-shirt that said *Kansas Motor Speedway* on it. "Dang it, man," he said. He shook his head and put his right hand to his neck as he walked to the rear of the car. "Dang it all."

Alan just wanted to give the guy his card so he could get on to the hospital. "Look, are you alright, sir? I can give you my card—"

"No, I ain't alright. Look at this," he yelled back, pointing at the dented silver bumper. It had come unhinged on one side and seemed to be hanging on by the grace of some unseen wad of chewing gum. How much of this was some previous accident's doing? Alan wondered. He'd barely tapped the guy. He looked back at the Benz and couldn't even see the scuff.

"I see that, but are you *okay*? Physically, sir?"

The man slowly turned his head to look at Alan, his expression saying he'd been asked maybe the dumbest question ever. "Cut out this 'sir' business." He took a step toward Alan, moving within a foot. It was too dark to see if his eyes were bloodshot. "You see me holding my neck, don't you? I'm hurt alright." The man leaned in even further, close to his face. Now Alan thought he could smell liquor on his breath, too. His teeth were crooked, yellow, leaning like old, untended tombstones.

"You've been drinking," Alan said. "You've been drinking and smoking marijuana."

"What'd you say?" the man said, pushing Alan lightly with the tips of his fingers. "You don't know anything about me. You're the one that hit *me*." Now he tapped his fingers hard against Alan's sternum. "So what are we gonna do about this, Mr. Mercedes?" He said this slowly, a cruel pleasure in the tone. He was right in Alan's face now and Alan understood what he was asking.

Alan should have removed the thick, crisp fold of bills from his leather wallet—a birthday gift that year from Sue—and casually palmed it into the man's hand and walked away, but he didn't. "I hope you're not proposing we swap cars."

"You think you're really fucking funny," he said, pushing Alan in the chest, harder this time. He fell off balance and stumbled back a few feet. Alan's could feel the beat of his heart in his ears. His chest was rising up and down quickly and suddenly—with this guy laughing at him—he felt a pointed anger pierce his middle. Something loosened within him and Alan charged. The man was already beginning to turn away, so that when Alan pushed him, the added force set the guy flying into the back of his own car. He slammed hard into the rear end and fell to the ground. He lay in the street, rolled over on his side, clutching his chest. A passing car flew by without stopping. The man groaned, holding his arm. "I just tapped you, was all. Was just playing around." His bark had softened, little more than a whimper.

Alan moved over and squatted next to him. "I'm sorry." He hadn't meant for this to happen. "Is it broken?" asked Alan, touching the man's arm, but the man jerked it away. "Let me take you to the hospital."

"Hospital?"

"I'm going there already. I'll drive you but we have to leave now."

"Don't need you to drive me. Besides, I ain't going there."

"You need to be checked out—"

"No insurance."

"What?"

"I. Do. Not. Have. Any. Insurance," the man said.

"I'll take care of that. I'm a doctor." The man grit his teeth, considering this a moment. Alan reached for his arm and he shook Alan off again. A few cars passed by, hurrying down the street. It was warm out—the real heat of summer would come soon. The man slowly stood up, looking like he still wasn't sure.

"Please," Alan said. "My father. He's at the hospital. He's dying."

The man laughed. "A minute ago you said it was your wife. Get your story straight before you go telling lies."

"I'm not. My father's dying and right now my wife's sitting at his bedside. With our son. They're waiting for me. I was stuck in surgery in Lawrence." He looked in the man's eyes. "He's not expected to make it through the night." The conviction with which he asserted this felt satisfying, earnest even. There was something about the lie that seemed to strike a chord with the man.

He kicked at the ground with the tip of his boot.

"Why'd you go and say something like that? Your dad, man? Shit," he said, apparently annoyed that he couldn't be angry. He looked at his arm, grimacing as he turned it, and finally agreed to follow Alan to the hospital.

As they approached the building, the blue plastic letters above the entranceway spelled out Emergency, reflecting the moon's luminous, full shape. They walked through the humid night to the heavy sliding doors of the entrance and moved inside. There the man stopped. He looked at Alan and pulled at his shirtsleeve. "You ain't gonna tell them about the weed, are you?"

Alan shook his head. "Wait here," he said and hurried over to the check-in desk, where a heavy black woman with dyed red hair sat behind a glass window. She looked like every middle-of-the-night E.R. nurse he could remember. He explained that he was a doctor and that the man needed to be looked at.

She glanced over Alan's shoulder at the man. "Looks okay to me."

"I'm the doctor. He needs medical attention."

"What he needs to do is fill this out," the woman said, shaking her head and handing him a patient information form. "He'll be next. You just take it easy, Dr. Lawson."

Alan motioned the man over to a row of orange, waiting-room seats where they sat down. His cell phone began to vibrate in his pocket. He looked at the screen. It was Lawrence Memorial. Sue. He didn't answer and in a few seconds the buzzing stopped. "You ain't gonna call the cops, are you? You ain't gonna leave me here, right?" Alan told him to fill out the form. He looked down at the paper as the man began to fill it out with his non-injured hand. There at the top of the page he saw the man's name: Terry. For a moment he thought he truly might stay with Terry, not wanting to face what awaited him deeper inside this massive building, hidden in a distant room. A muted TV was replaying the late local news about a shooting downtown. Several half-full Styrofoam cups littered the tables, resting on top of creased magazines, and there was only the sound of Terry's labored script pressing hard on the paper. Fear began to pinwheel inside Alan's stomach, and he felt as he often had back in Seattle as a resident on an emergency case he'd never handled before. He thought of the first patient he'd ever lost, a monstrously obese man who ate until the staples in his stomach pulled out and Alan, elbow deep inside the man's distended belly, couldn't temper the shock that had overwhelmed his system; he saw Greenleaf's fading blue iris, disappearing below an opaque cornea; then his father's face that last night at the med center, staring at him with a cold eye. The baby would be dead, a small, still, blue body wrapped in a blanket.

"Done," Terry said, thrusting the paper Alan's way. He had an amused look on his face.

"What?' Alan said.

Terry shook his head slowly. "You're a doctor, right? And we're in a hospital." He scanned the room. "Well, now this is just funny, ain't it?"

Alan looked around the E.R. There was no one else there. No one needing care. He couldn't remember a night in Seattle when it hadn't seemed there were an endless stream of emergencies, kids with broken arms, junkies with eyes rolled back in their heads, and guys with pulped-out faces from bar fights leaning against walls because there was no space left to sit. As he took Terry's paperwork to the counter, his phone began to vibrate again. "Leave the form here and a doctor will be with him shortly," the woman said from rote, eyes fixed on her computer screen.

He held the paper out until she looked up and met his eyes. "Where is the newborn intensive care unit?"

"Neonatal?" the woman said, a surprised kindness seeming to come over her.

Alan looked to his left, down a long, bright corridor and was already moving in that direction before she could answer. Behind him he could hear Terry's voice call after him, echoing in the empty room. He kept walking, the phone buzzing madly in his pocket. He didn't know where he was going, but it felt important to be moving. Eventually he would find his way and enter the room where his son was barely living or already dead. If he were alive, Alan would spend the night praying for the boy's survival, to a god all practical experience had taught him to doubt, and if he were dead, Alan would ask to see him so he could hold the boy in his arms and really look at him, so that when Sue asked he'd be able to tell her what their son had been like.

Ulysses

"OH GOODY," she says from behind the check-in desk, looking at my arms. "They're gonna love you over there. I could wait all day and not see veins like these." Having stood in line for nearly two hours I feel like I have been waiting all day, but I just smile and say, "There sure are a lot of people." She tussles papers around, then looks up suddenly. "You're doing a great thing," she says, touching my arm. Her latex gloves make me think of condoms, but she's old, and a lady, and the thought is sinister. She hands me a form and tells me to fill it out, so I shuffle over to the crowded waiting room and find a single empty seat.

"Volunteering," the man in the neighboring chair says to no one in particular as he looks at the others already on their backs. He has on a mesh-backed hat with a bald eagle on it and a too-tight shirt with the words *The Sunflower State* stretching across his belly. He holds his form loosely in one hand and with the other jingles the loose change in his pocket each time he takes a deep breath. I begin to think he's watching me, so I cover my form with my hand, the way kids used to do during exams. I pause on question 17: Have you ever had sex with a man before 1977? Why would they ask that?

Old Condom Hands moseys over for a drink of water and sees me sitting, looking at the form. "Do you have any questions?" she inquires.

"My mom," I say, "she used to get bruises from doing it too often, too many times. Terrible looking things, up and down her whole arm."

"That sometimes happens when people donate too frequently. When did you last give?" she asks.

"Never," I say, and she laughs, touching my arm. I can feel her frozen skin through the latex gloves and hope she won't be the one putting the needle in. "But those bruises," I say, as she riffles through her pockets for something. "Terrible." She pulls out a sticker and slaps it on my chest, smiling. Be nice to me, it's my first time—that's what the sticker says, but upside-down it looks like a fancy foreign language.

When I drove by the bank's electronic sign earlier, on my way here, it said eighty-nine degrees, but inside it's much cooler, and here now, cooler still. There's a TV in the corner of the room showing all the things that made me leave the trailer in the first place. Over and over. Images. A never-ending ticker, scrolling. I look away from the screen and down at my form.

Soon a group of them walk me over to a table near the others, asking me which arm. I point to my right. "Alright then," they say, "lie down with your head at that end. Take a deep breath. Just a little prick," they whisper. I'm by a window and turn to look out, watching a group of gnats, small as baby toenails, circle a tree bough. They give me a red ball and tell me to squeeze it, that it helps circulate the blood. There's a sharp pain followed by an uncomfortable pressure as they fumble the needle once, and I think back to this kid I knew in school who was sick with diabetes and had to prick his fingers a dozen times a day, it seemed. We both rode the same bus—the rural one, smaller than the others—to the consolidated school here in Ulysses because our towns were so small they didn't have high schools. There were a few others who drew our lot, kids from towns that were unincorporated or had only a few hundred people, but they pretty much kept to themselves. The "hick bus," everyone called it, and we obliged, unknowingly, wearing our overalls and ill-fitting clothes that had been passed through entire litters of family members.

He was pretty fat, this kid, and taller than me too, because he was older—he'd been held back a couple years on account of missing so much time with his illness. We were friendly, I suppose, taking turns accepting fists and feet that were meant for the other's chest or genitals. For this reason we stuck close, even used to sneak off to the bathroom together whenever he had to check his blood. I used to keep watch on the door to see if someone was gonna come in. But one time, as he held the pinched flab of his side together to receive the needle, he stopped and asked if I wanted to do it for him. He'd lifted his shirt, exposing his massive belly, the blue and yellow stripes that ringed his briefs. I took the pin and leaned close to his side. But then, glancing up and seeing the look on his face—eyes shut, jawbone popping—I froze, unable to stick it in. I could feel it coming inside me and shortly began to cry, as I was often given to do. He said it was okay, asked why I was crying, and then hugged me. I was surprised and tried to pull away, but he held me tight. His voice was soft, seemed almost small coming from such a big body. I sniffled, mewling, unable to make the words come that should have said, *Because I'm fifteen years old and still a crybaby; because I'm smaller than everyone else and no one likes me; because my daddy didn't come back from the war and my mom won't leave the trailer,* but I just pulled away. It seemed like a semester of school might have passed, a thousand-something needle pricks, before he spoke again. He said there was nothing to be scared of, that he was okay, that he was going to be fine, and then reached for my arm to help me raise the needle. But then the door opened and an older kid walked in—"What are you faggots doing in here?"—and I ran out of the bathroom, down the hallway, leaving him to take the beating alone this time.

There are ten or so of us, horizontal, feeding the leech machines. That's as many as they can take at one time, I gather. I look back at the waiting room and see that it's still packed. The people waiting all have their long, worried faces on and can't stop from watching the television, the same way my mom couldn't when I told her I was coming down here. I said, "Mama, I'm gonna take the truck and drive to Ulysses, go give some blood"—like I'd heard someone on the television suggest, because what could anyone in Kansas really do? She said, "How's all that blood gonna get to New York?" and when I said they have smarter people than me who figure out such things and that she should come with me, she just sat there in the same purple nightgown she's been wearing for weeks without saying a word, eyes stuck on the screen.

I look at the others around me. Old and young. Man and woman. There's a guy nearby lying with his head opposite mine and I maneuver to see his face, which makes my arm hurt a little, but I do it anyway. I try to smile, but when he sees me staring at him he looks away, so I turn my head towards the window.

They come over and look at my bag. "You're three-quarters there," they say. "Don't forget to squeeze the ball every once in a while." I shut my eyes, listen to the hum of the fan above me, and envision it circling in my head. A minute later, they come back and say, "You're all set here. Take a deep breath while we pull it out." I open my eyes. The iodine on my arm looks like bile and I feel the upsetness in my stomach. It's not the needle so much as seeing the bag that really does a number on me. They rest it next to me like an arm that has just fallen off, like a tick fit to explode. For a moment I want to pick it up and run for the door. "What are you going to do with this?" I ask, looking down at it. "We're going to save a life, sir," they say, and take it away from me.

They tell me that I should eat something and walk me over to where the old folks from the senior center have volunteered to pass out food and drink. When I see what they give you, I'd almost have done it just for the food. A whole spread of sandwiches, bagels, crackers, and beverages lie cold on a brown foldout table. The old people talk and sometimes I answer or comment, mostly just listen though, the way I do back at the trailer on nights my mom—one room over, separated only by a thin layer of drywall—can't sleep, still mumbling about my dad. I should grab something for her, some cookies or a juice box for that sweet-tooth of hers, but I don't because the old people keep tabs on what's been eaten on their big click board. I try to talk to them, wanting to hear more about their grandkids in Liberal and Meade, Ashland and Dodge City. But soon they run out of family members to tell me about, pictures to share. When the long spell of silence gets to me, I open a second package of crackers and smile, saying, "All this donating is hard work," trying to say something that makes a bad day a little easier, but by now they don't smile, just look away. I glance at the clock on the wall, then at the TV, still going. I don't want to leave yet, though, is the thing. Not ready to. I consider falling to the floor and saying I'm too lightheaded to drive so I can stay, but by my third orange juice they start with the looks that say they're very much ready for me to go. "There are so many others waiting," a woman with wiry gray hair, just like my mom's, finally says, looking back at the others nearby. I snatch a last package of crackers and jump out of my chair quickly.

Ulysses—that was the kid's name, same as the town we traveled to for high school, this very one that has accepted my blood. Being that they lived so close to Grant County, his mom had liked the presidential ring to it, expecting great things from her son, but her whim only dug the hole deeper for him. It was a name people liked hearing themselves say. It sounded through the halls at school in taunts and jeers: "Ulysses S. Fat" was one of their favorites. And when their classes were reading the old books, "Ulysses, how's Penelope?" they'd call after us, laughing, as we walked to class, meaning me when they said Penelope, thinking us amorous. "You still lost? Ain't you found your way home yet, Ulysses?" Even at night I could still hear their voices as I lay in bed, waiting for sleep to come. He never said a word about it though, only asked me to call him Uli, so I obliged him that.

He died a few years later when we were seniors, almost done with the whole damn thing. Uli. We used to sit in the back of our bus and I'd watch as he'd maneuver to prick himself with that awful needle. The kid could do it on a bus humping dirt roads at sixty miles an hour. He would get dropped off a ways before me in Big Bow, which always made the ride to my stop in Manter, another twenty minutes on, feel like a long while yet.

One morning he wasn't on the bus when I got on, which wasn't unusual with his condition, but then the next day an announcement came crackling over the school's speakers, right after the pledge of allegiance, telling us all about Uli. Later that week as I was getting on the bus to go home, Mr. Malick, the driver, said, "Where's your friend?" I stood there looking at him, silent, blinking. I could feel it coming, my eyes moving to water. I couldn't tell if he was making fun of me like the kids did or not, but it didn't matter. "The big one," he said, "gets off in Big Bow. Hasn't been on all week." I didn't move, trying to find some words to say without blubbering so. "He wasn't my friend," I said, wiping at my sissy eyes, scratching, and shouldered my bag a little as I walked to the back. I didn't want to go home. I wanted to get on the bus and never get off, just ride forever, flat out leave, watch the squares of country divided by grain elevators and windmills pass outside my window. I slumped into the empty seat and let my body ease into the new space, shaking a little from the bus's trembling idle, waiting for the long ride past miles of short-grassed prairie to start.

Outside now, after I leave, the air sticks to me and in the truck it's worse, burning my skin, but when I drive by the bank on my way back to Manter, to the melting trailer, to the insane television, to Mama, the sign now says eighty-eight degrees; one degree cooler.

The Cure for Cancer

BEFORE SHE WAS DIAGNOSED—before the disease—my sister drove up from Lawrence to help me move into my new apartment in Kansas City, to "keep tabs on her little brother," she said. It had always been her joke, that I was younger than her, seemingly since she came out of the womb thirteen months before me. I had just moved back to the area after two aborted attempts at law school in Iowa City. In an effort to erase some of my college debt I applied for and, still to my mild surprise, accepted a teaching assignment at an underfunded inner-city junior high school in Kansas City, Kansas. The *other* Kansas City. A rough neighborhood, I knew, not like the suburb where Carol and I grew up, but it was only for two years and I'd be close to my sister. We would both teach.

She came to stay for four days during the last week before the start of classes, helping me unpack boxes and furnish the apartment. It was the heat of summer, and I'd awkwardly hefted up my window unit to find it was too big for the small windows of my new apartment. Carol laughed it off, in typical fashion, and we spent ensuing afternoons in chilly movie theaters, watching comedic matinees, wrists drooped over the rims of gigantic tubs of popcorn.

Carol lived with her husband Dan in Lawrence, where he worked in H.R. at a growing insurance company. They had a six-year-old son, Sam, my nephew. Carol had made a career as a permanent adjunct of introductory English classes, bouncing around from college to college for shitty pay. But she loved it. "Where else but the adjunct circuit can your students mistakenly refer to you as 'Doctor So-and-so' when you only have a masters?" she said. "Besides no bullshit committee work. No departmental meetings. I have freedom." The best part was that she was able to design her own classes, so she always taught Shakespeare, her first love, showing the kids how to wrestle with the language, pointing out all the bawdy puns. She only taught the tragedies, she said, because at the very least the kids needed those.

On our final night together, I was unpacking a box, the last I would for a number of months, and found something I'd forgotten about: a slide projector. It had been our parents', loaded with pictures from when they were first married, before Carol and I had been born. Our parents had us late, not until Mom was forty-one. My father had an almost perverse affinity for documentation, part of the reason he'd been such a good lawyer. More often than not, mental images I conjure of him include some kind of camera at his side or to his eye, eclipsing half his face. I looked down at the projector, so old and oversized, and showed Carol. Her eyes got big, and she clapped her hands together—"Pictures!"—speeding to the kitchen, where she filled two glasses with white wine from the box in my fridge. I set the projector on a card table and propped it up with a dictionary. When it clicked on, a beam of light shot through the motes of dust drifting singly like flakes of snow; the stuff you never realize, I thought. We spent the rest of the night getting toasty on cheap wine and watching pictures of our parents slide over my blank, white wall, pictures from when they had fallen in love—not the unhappiness, obesity and disease of middle age and retirement, but a time when they were younger, before life had imploded. In the dark silence of my new apartment I saw my parents come back to life, image by image for only a second, to a time before Carol and I had been alive.

"How old are they here?" I asked.

"Early-mid thirties, I think," Carol answered. She was sitting on the floor, the beam hovering a few feet above her head. Her back was to me and periodically when an image struck her she'd reach behind and grab my foot, momentarily latching onto it and shaking excitedly.

We, too, were nearly halfway through that decade. It's a strange thing to see your parents at the same age as you, all of their authority and distance shrinks away and they might just be folks you pass on the street, as hopeful and lost as you.

"I can't believe they were together for so long," I said. "Before they had us, I mean. What the hell did they do all the time?"

"Lord only knows," she shook her head, taking a sip from the clear plastic cups we were both using. Then she reached for my foot again— "Look"—and laughed, pointing at the next picture. It was one of our father. On his way to some costume party. He was in rare form: dressed in a cowboy hat with a fake handlebar mustache, smiling that cautious smile he seldom let himself indulge in, a look that seemed to suggest, *I know I'm above this, but it's okay to let your hair down once in a while . . . once in a while.* He was still alive, but today there were only words, not images, by which to construct him: wheelchair, Florida, Alzheimer's, nursing home. They floated around my head like a mobile of planets whenever I thought of him. Our mother had died in her sleep three years before. Afterwards, our father moved to Florida, where his brain began the slow process of forgetting itself.

I received the call from Carol nearly a month later as I was struggling with my new teaching position. I hadn't taught since I was in graduate school (the first time), and the crash course certification program I'd completed the previous summer was mostly an overview of what to do if a student came to class armed or on drugs. These kids were eating me alive: I couldn't control them; they didn't respect me; they hated the material. I told Carol so and she laughed, the old veteran. Her classes at the community college were going "swimmingly," she said with a British accent. "But they are, you know, college students," she added in her normal voice. She offered advice, jokes mostly, games I could try, and if that failed there was always mental abuse and humiliation. "Oh for the days of the belt and lash," she sighed, wistful. My mind wandered off as Carol continued. I imagined being one of my students, sitting in a classroom with all the other black children, staring up at an awkward white man delivering stale one-liners, trying to rouse anything from the void of the sleepy and confused. *I just flew in from Iowa City and boy are my arms tired. Try the roast beef. Tip your waitress. I'll be here all week, or until my loans are paid off.* When I came back to, she was telling me about going to the doctor recently to have her breast examined. She had found a lump, she said so matter-of-factly.

"A lump?" I said.

She told me not to interrupt, she was telling a story. "So they bring me in the room, the examination room, you know. And the doctor— this squirrelly looking guy with a goatee—tells me to take my shirt off and lie down on my stomach. And I'm thinking, I'd bet you'd like that now wouldn't you. But I do it, good girl that I am. Now the table, you should have seen it. The table has a hole right where my boob is. And I sort of look back at the nurse, and she gives a look like, yes, sweetie, drop it right in there. So I do. Bombs away. It was like one of those cutouts at an amusement park—where you stick your face through a hole to have your picture taken, so it looks like you're a cowboy or a huge body builder. Something like that." I found myself nodding, thinking, Lump. "But it gets better. Then he hits a button and the table starts to elevate, like I'm a car at the repair shop, and I tell him to give the tires a rotation while he's down there, but he doesn't say much. Just whispers something to the nurse. And then finally he goes underneath to examine my disembodied boob," she said. "The little perv," she giggled.

I knew then what was happening and what would happen, could see the whole terrible future in a millisecond. I imagine some part of Carol did too, but she stayed calm. "It's no big deal," she said, "so don't go getting all maudlin on me." I thought of how after Mom died people told me she was in a better place. And when my uncle Terry had survived his first tumor biopsy—before they began to fresco his whole upper torso—everyone said what a fighter he was. This, the language of coping.

I had called him, my uncle Terry, the day after that first operation, at my mother's urging. I was young and she had to dial the number for me. When he answered, woozy from pain pills, the first thing I asked was if he was going to die. Mom snatched the phone from my hand. "He means, how are you feeling?" and gave the phone back to me. There was a delay, perhaps he was gathering himself, before he answered: "I feel pretty good for having my throat slit yesterday."

It all happens so quickly, the blink of an eye, the turn of your head:

After the mammogram, the biopsy, the modified radical mastectomy, and the chemo, there is a recurrence. Her oncologist calls it a "local recurrence," which means, he tells us, looking each one of us in the eye, that the cancerous tumor cells remained in the original site. I picture one of those time-elapsed films of flowers blooming. Usually, when this happens, the tumor grows back over a long period of time; this is abnormally quick. He recommends a hospital in Omaha that specializes in cancer treatment, where things are "top notch." Within the month Carol is relocated to Omaha. Because she's from out of town, she stays at the hospital full-time (unlike most of her fellow patients who arrive for treatment and leave again), while Dan takes care of Sammy in Lawrence and looks for an apartment to rent in Omaha. The first time I make the three-and-a-half-hour drive north from Kansas City I get lost, spacing off at the snow-covered barns I pass in the early winter afternoon. I miss a sign and end up on another highway, nearly halfway to Iowa City, before realizing the error and turning around.

In the hospital I stop four separate doctors for directions, check in at three different desks, and present my driver's license a handful of times before being given her room number and a clip-on badge that makes it undoubtedly clear I am in fact a FAMILY VISITOR. Walking the halls toward Carol's room, I feel uncomfortable in the same way airports make me uneasy: the hustle and bustle; the worried and reunited families with their Styrofoam cups of coffee, milling about, aimless as cattle; the slow walks that explode into sprint at the hint of urgency. And the smell, that sanitized smell my brain can only further characterize as sickly, as nauseating as the smell of jet fuel that forces me to breathe out of my nose whenever I queue up in that discouragingly long line, waiting to find my seat assignment.

I find her room, 44, and enter. She is in bed with one leg on top of her blanket. There is a box of Kleenex by her left leg and a mound of clumped tissues beside her right thigh. A small army of machines surrounds her, the clear tubing winding all over her body. She's in the middle of treatment. They have decided to try chemo and radiation concurrently, hoping for what her doctor calls "synergism." She is alone, reading. She stares intently at the page and doesn't seem to notice me. For a moment I think about turning around and leaving, driving back to Kansas City. I want no part of this. My palm slides behind my back, latching onto the door handle, ready to slowly turn and walk out. But then I'm spotted when Carol laughs at a passage in her book and looks up, eyeing me in a quizzical manner.

"What are you doing skulking around like that, Kojak?"

I take a few steps toward her. "Didn't want to disturb you."

She nods, slowly and suspiciously.

I take off my jacket and sling it onto a chair that has a stack of magazines on it.

"Welcome to my new abode," she says, lifting one arm over her head. The tubes hanging off it slap against each other, and she winces a little.

"How do you like it here?"

"It's shitty and small," she answers, which makes me look around the room. "And yet," she says, "I believe it's still bigger than your apartment."

I laugh, exhaling harder than I mean to.

I tell her how tough it was getting clearance to visit. "It's like you're top secret," I say. "I'm lucky I didn't have to take a blood test to get in here."

She purses her lips and makes the face she always does when I try to be funny. It is the face of a parent touched by her child's effort.

"What are you reading?"

"Dante," she says, flipping over the book and showing me the cover. "I'm in purgatory now." She points to the cover. "Just finished the *Inferno*. I want to complete the Comedy before—" she's saying when her oncologist walks in with his head in a chart.

"Doctor Kim, this is my brother Jacob," Carol says, affecting a dramatic English accent, "bastard son of the Earl of Gloucester." She does this sometimes, slips into Shakespeare.

The doctor looks at me, confused or interested I can't tell, as if to say *She's been doing this since she arrived. What does it mean?*

Doctor Kim sidles around in constant conversation with himself, flipping charts and clicking pens. After he leaves I ask her what she thinks of him. She blows her nose. "Well, he's Chinese," she says, waving a hand as if this explains everything. She refers to anyone with roots in an Asian country as Chinese, an atavism from our grandfather, who lived well into his nineties and never understood the whole P.C. thing. When I tell her I think he's Korean, she just snorts and looks away: "Why are you so uptight all the time?"

She blows her nose again and tosses the tissue into the pile. It's silent, and I feel the need to say something either funny or hopeful. She sniffs and her nose makes a little whistle sound. She ignores it, and starts thumbing the corners of her book, looking at me, squinting like she's trying to decide whether to tell me something really important. But when it happens again, the little whistle, she starts to laugh which in turn makes her do it more. Then she stops. "Listen. 'Twinkle Twinkle Little Star,'" she says, and puts her hands up to her nose, pressing her nostrils open and closed.

Stacks of unpacked boxes still line the corners of my apartment, shrinking my already small living space. It feels like some Lego construction gone terribly wrong, like instead of building up or out I'm growing in, confining myself to the smallest possible space. When I need something from one of the boxes, I remove it from the stack, take out the item, and put the box back where it was. Three months and I can't bring myself to fully settle. After school I come home to make dinner and then have to leave again. I spend most nights going to bars or bookstores, drinking things that either speed me up or slow me down. Some nights, though, I just walk around all night. I live in a poor neighborhood, full of liquor stores and government housing, not far from school, a condition of the teaching deal I accepted. Usually, I drive past State Line, crossing into the Missouri side of Kansas City. There I walk downtown under the golden and red pulse of the flashing Western Auto sign, where abandoned buildings and bankrupt businesses are being turned into galleries, trendy gay bars, and lofts.

Tonight though, Friday, it's freezing so I decide to stay close, to walk to school and see what it looks like at night, empty. I pull on my wool hat and zip the parka that saw me through several Iowa winters unscathed. The waning evening light gives way to the click of streetlights that illuminate perfect circles of pavement. Illegally parked cars block hydrants and spill over curbs, their owners unconcerned that the police will make their way over here. People crowd around the doorways and stoops of ramshackle buildings. I walk by one house where there's a party going on. Loud thumping music crackles out the windows. From the street the bass feels like the initial tremors of a coming earthquake. Groups pack the porches, smoking and drinking from red plastic cups. I fear bumping into one of my students out here, or, worse, their parents. Cars pass me slowly, writhing from all the bass. I can feel my lungs shake. Sore thumb that I am, which is to say white and dressed in khakis, my neighbors can't help but notice me. I stuff my hands into my pockets, trying to get them warm, and can feel the rings of my nostrils beginning to freeze. The voices pick up on both sides of the street as I walk past. Laughter and catcalls fly around the air.

Someone says something to me now, closer, and I keep walking, head down.

"Where you think you're going?"

I keep on, hoping he'll leave me alone if I just walk fast enough. He speeds up and I can feel him just a few paces back.

"Hey, white shadow, you in the wrong part of town?"

My fists clinch inside my pockets.

"You separated from the herd, little white lamb?"

I hear the people from nearby porches yelling things I can't make out.

"No," I say. "I live here."

Then I feel his hand on my shoulder.

"Hey!" he pulls harder and I stop.

"Don't you know where you are, white shadow?"

I look at the ground. He has on big black boots with cleatlike treads.

"Kansas City, Kansas," I say. A moment passes and then I hear laughter and look up to find him doubled over. He's gasping for air.

"Yeah," he laughs, "yeah, you is." Then he turns around and starts yelling to the others on the porch and it's hysterical pandemonium. "You hear what he say?" I walk away slowly. "You should come party with us, man," he calls after me. "For real, we could use some laughs." I put my hands back in my pocket, the comedian, and walk on toward school.

———————

I arrive in Omaha in the midst of a huge winter storm. It's before the roads have turned muddy with slush, and everything seems disconcertingly placid, a deathly calm all over town. A few cars venture out, seemingly to just *be* out in this. I want to pull over, get out of the car, and look at the sky so I can feel small against it all. But instead I drive. Carol waits, growing thinner, losing hair, weight. I continue plowing up side streets—one of the tricks I've learned by now—to the back entrance of the hospital. I turn the key, the engine goes quiet, and for a moment it's just my breath. As I get out, my foot sinks several inches before touching the ground, and snow slips into my shoe.

Inside, I now walk with the purpose of one who belongs. I nod to the familiar faces whose shifts coincide with my weekly visits. When I arrive, I find Dan sitting in a chair by Carol's bed, holding Sammy in his lap. It's one of the few times I've seen Dan here. Carol says he's been busy holding things together in Lawrence.

Sammy explodes out of Dan's lap.

"Uncle Jacob," he says.

"Call him 'Nuncle,' Sammy," Carol says. She's been reading *Lear* again, her favorite, making notes, still convinced she'll be back teaching next fall. I give her a muddled grin and move over to her bedside to kiss her head.

"When it all falls out, I want you to call me 'Curly,' okay?"

"Sure, sis. Curly," I say, standing up. I walk over to the other side of the bed, Sammy hanging on my leg, and shake hands with Dan. Carol has told me of the stress he feels, but to me he looks less frazzled than numb—someone already defeated.

On the phone earlier in the week, Carol asked me if I'd take Sammy out for a while. "He's had a tough time with it all," she said. She told me that the last time Sammy came to visit he scraped his knee and instead of coming to her as usual he ran right past her into Dan's arms. "He's already learning how to live without me." I asked her if she had any suggestions about where I take him. "I don't know. Something fun. There's supposed to be a great zoo here in town. Dan will be looking for apartments, and I don't want Sammy to have to sit here and watch me in treatment."

Used tissues still decorate her bed. She brings a fresh one up to her nose. In the quiet of the room the sound is arresting. "Out, out damned snot!" she says in her best Elizabethan and suddenly we're all laughing, relieved. There is an awkward moment after we've caught our breath when the three of us stare at each other, unsure what to do next. Thankfully Sammy tugs at my belt: "Nuncle, Nuncle, pick me up." I do, and Dan slumps down in a chair, looking like a general relieved of duty. He was always quiet, but now seems almost speechless. I remember when he and Carol were dating and she thought he was the one. She wanted me to go out with him and get to know him, to see what I thought, so one night Dan and I went to a sports bar near my parents' house in Overland Park, south of the city. We spent the first twenty minutes getting acquainted the best that two introverts can. We were like amputees trying to shake hands. We ordered beers and managed to smile at one another, nodding, but gradually our eyes drifted to two of the ubiquitously placed televisions, and for the next hour we watched the Royals blow a huge lead in the ninth, muttering things like *shit* and *what else is new* under our breath. Afterwards I dropped Dan off at his car and went to Carol's apartment, where she was waiting up for me. "Well, what do you think?" she asked, so damn excited, falling into my arms. "I think he's great," I said, embracing her.

"How was the drive?" Carol asks now.

"The storm was heavy, but the driving's not too bad."

"Storm?"

"Several inches of snow."

"I didn't even realize," she says, looking across the room at the window. "Sort of in my own world up here." She watches the snow a few seconds longer. "Guess the zoo is out."

———

Sammy insists on sitting in the back. I check to see that he has put on his seat belt and then turn around. He has one of those old winter hats with the floppy ears that makes him look like a basset hound. I turn the ignition and adjust the vent settings for defrost. Then, putting the car in reverse, I hear: "Quit looking at me!" My foot hits the brake, and I check the rearview. He's just sitting there.

"I'm not looking at you, Sam," I say, though, of course, now I am.

"I'm not talking to you," he says, "I'm talking to *him*," pointing at the empty seat next to him.

"There's nothing there, Sam."

He seems to almost chuckle at my ignorance, twisting the corduroy of his pant leg between thumb and forefinger. "George is hiding from you."

I look at him, and he looks over at George. I put the car in reverse again and we're off. The snow is still coming down. I have no idea what to do, so I drive around the city until we're both hungry. In McDonald's Sammy nibbles on his hamburger and fries, patiently searching for his toy in the Happy Meal. I struggle for conversation. Without much of my own doing he's always seemed to like me, something I've never quite learned how to deal with. I hadn't been to visit much during his first few years, while I was in school, but whenever I came back at Christmas he always followed me around, asking questions, mimicking the way I walked. Carol had told him stories about me, she said, and I wondered, *What stories?*

"No toy," he says, turning the box upside down. A lone soggy fry falls onto his tray. "No toy, Nuncle."

This is my moment, I realize, to be the cool uncle and fix things. "Hang on," I say, standing up, full of gusto, and march to the counter. And with visions of making a big scene on behalf of my young nephew—*whose mother has cancer, I'll have you know*—possibly garnering Sammy an extra toy and an earnest apology, I choke and inform the young, pimpled manager that there is a toy missing from that little boy's meal over there. Silently, I accept what he slides across the counter as he hands over a large fry to another customer: a small figurine in a plastic baggie.

"Here you go," I say, putting the toy down in front of Sammy.

"Thanks, Nuncle."

"You don't really have to call me that," I say, but he is busy burrowing into the plastic. He pulls out the toy and looks at it quizzically. Then he smiles and sets it on the table before the seat next to him. "How long have you and George been friends?" I ask. He tells me four months. I nod, finishing the last of my burger, doing the math in my head. It makes sense, I realize, counting backwards to the first phone call with Carol, and suddenly I understand, feeling the gulf in my middle expanding, watching as he tries to get George to play with the figurine.

After he finishes, we return to the car and I take the wheel with a sense of urgency. He asks where we're going and I tell him it's a surprise. Snowflakes hit the windshield and for a split second I see the gossamer before the wipers erase them. When we arrive, I park and open his door. The parking lot is nearly empty. Plowed hours ago, the snow has reclaimed the stretch of pavement. We walk hand in hand until he sees where we are and takes off in a little sprint. I tell him to slow down, and he looks back—at me or George, I can't tell—and continues on. He runs inside through the huge automatic doors—"Come on, Nuncle"—waving his hand at me, and I start to get caught up in it, too. I remember being his age and I begin to trot, finally catching up with him inside near the board games. I look at the titles that flash by as we move. It's one of those mega-toy stores, so the games seem to stretch from the floor to the distant heavens. Because of the storm it's empty. He motors on, around corners and up every aisle, past the videogames and through the sporting goods. He stops in the action figures though, the rows and colors of the packaging overwhelming. He stands there, calm, looking up at the superheroes and wrestlers, soldiers and cartoon characters. There's a cart nearby that someone has abandoned, and I walk over and grab it. I reach for a figure and drop it into the cart. He watches me do this, and when our eyes meet some unspoken understanding seems to occur, and seconds later we're both pouring toys into the cart. I watch to see which figure he grabs and then start piling in others from the set. Then we're off, running again for some reason, going up every aisle and putting things in the cart that Sammy wants: games, cap guns, balls, a wiffleball bat, cheap electronic things that say the same thing over and over.

When I finally make it up to the checkout line, the cashier eyes me like, *It's because of assholes like you that I have to be here now.* She laboriously takes every item from the cart and slides them under the scanner. At the moment I don't care about money, so when the small digital screen comes up with $686.09, I calmly reach for my wallet, not batting an eye.

We return to the hospital and find Carol alone, rolled over on her side. I think she's sleeping, so we tiptoe in. The gigantic bags under my arms begin to crackle, the plastic squeals.

"Who doth enter the hearth?"

"Just us," I say, as I set the bags down on the floor.

"Good, I thought you were one of them coming to prod the Body," she says, turning over on to her back. "What have you all been up to?" she says, grimacing and then smiling when she catches a glimpse of the bags.

"A little shopping."

She looks tired, not sleepy but weary. Her voice is softer. "Did you and Nuncle have a good time?"

Sammy nods, coming over to the side of her bed, and rests his head on her chest, where her right breast used to be. She runs her hand through his hair. He moves his head a little and I see Carol wince. There's a legal pad by her bed with her script all over it and two books, *Lear* and *Il Paradiso*. "Look, I made it to heaven," she says, nudging the Dante. One of Michelangelo's from the Sistine Chapel adorns the cover. I ask her what it's all about, pointing at the notepad. "I'm writing my autobiography," she says, flipping the legal pad over so I can't see anything. "I always wanted to write a book, but I could never get past the title. I had zillions of those, but no story. Now I know what story I want to tell." She pauses, then chuckles to herself: "Spoken like a true narcissist." I ask her where she's at in her narrative and she says, "The title," and shrugs sheepishly. "I only just started this afternoon." She winces again, as though absorbing a blow to the stomach none of us can see, and tells me they've switched her medication again. Something called Tamoxifen. "They call it an 'adjustment,'" she says, making her fingers into a pair of bunny ears. "I don't see what was wrong with the old stuff, but these people . . ." she starts, but her thought dies mid sentence. "I'll adjust them." She looks down at her chest. "Mommy needs to roll over," she tells Sammy, gently lifting his head.

Sammy backs away from the bed and goes over to the chair where the Coke and lollipop I bought him await. He takes a swig of pop and sets the can down, going right for the sucker. He looks at Carol and then goes to the middle of the room and starts doing a funny little dance he does whenever he wants to make her laugh. She watches him, mustering a smile, but her eyes begin to shut and she rolls onto her other side, away from us. Sammy's shuffling his feet and hopping around, his lollipop in his mouth. "Look at me!" he shouts.

Carol rolls back over, leans forward as much as she can and shouts, "Sam!" He's still trying to dance his jig. "Don't jump around with that in your mouth!" Then, calmer: "You might choke, honey." Sammy stops and takes the little white stick out of his mouth. He walks over to the chair and slumps into it, grasping his Coke with two hands and raising it to his mouth.

Dan arrives as I'm flipping through channels on a television that's attached to the ceiling like a security camera. Sammy's having a conversation with George about the toys we bought. Dan bends over and kisses Carol. He says nobody was available to show him the apartments because of the storm. I look at him, confused, half wanting to ask if he actually thought anybody would be, but then I understand. I see it in his eyes; he needed to leave. We shake hands and he says hello to Sammy, who looks up for a moment and then goes back to talking with George. "Say hello to Daddy, Sam," Carol says, still on her side so her words come out mashed. Sammy keeps on talking, holding up the plastic yellow bat. Carol exhales and leans off the pillow. "For Christ's sake, Sammy, George isn't real," she says. Sammy's eyes go big as sunflowers and his mouth opens like he's waiting for someone to place an egg in it. "This is real," she cries, and drops back down to the bed, covering her face.

That night I can't stand it. I have to leave. I need to get out of the hospital and see people I don't know, people who don't have cancer or imaginary friends. I get in my car and drive to the Old Market. It's midnight and I pull in front of the first dive I find. It's a country bar and everyone has on cowboy shirts and Wranglers. There's cheap champagne on tap and schooners of beer as big as fishbowls. I make a resolution to drink as much as I can before close. I settle down at a table with two Millers and watch the couples slow dance. The men in cowboy hats stare into their partners' eyes and sing along to the saccharine ballads. For the second round I order a Boilermaker. Soon I begin to feel it in my toes, and I find myself swaying as song dissolves into song. Sometimes they're slow and other times fast. After I order my last drink, the mustachioed bartender leans over the rail and screams last call. Then the lights dim further and a song everyone seems to know comes on. All the women in the bar walk onto the dance floor. They move into formation, three or four horizontal lines, each knowing exactly where to go. And then the dance begins. It's slow at first, their smiles concealing a deep concentration, and they move in synch, step for step—line dancing. I watch them turn and spin all together with the precision of a professional outfit, and they are beautiful, moving as one. I raise the pint to my lips, and catching the eyes of the other men in the crowd I see what it is to love and know that it will never be enough to save us.

———————

Dan answers the door like I'm a Jehovah's Witness. He looks through a four-inch crack between door and frame.

"How's it going?" I say.

He looks at me a moment longer, then says, "Fine," and opens the door a little more. "Doing fine."

Perhaps I shouldn't have just shown up like this. The look in his eye tells me this. We stand there like two gunfighters, waiting for the other to make the slightest move. It's quiet. My breath freezes as it leaves my mouth, floating towards him, and disappears as it drifts into the house. I look at my feet. The doormat, sandy with old winter, says *Welcome.*

"Can I come in?"

"Sure."

Inside I notice he's wearing a red tattered bathrobe, Carol's. He knocks a box off a chair in the living room. "Excuse the mess," he says. There are half-packed boxes everywhere. I haven't been here since Carol went to Omaha, months ago.

"No work today?" I ask.

He keeps looking out the window every few seconds.

"I'm taking some time," he says. This explains so much and so little.

I pull off my winter hat and unzip my jacket. My hair is standing straight up with static. He looks at me like I'm insane.

"Are you going to Omaha tonight?"

"I don't know. There's still an awful lot to do around here," he says.

"I thought maybe we could all go up together. You, me, and Sammy."

"Sammy's in school now."

"I mean when he finishes. We could all grab a bite to eat and head up. I'll drive."

He nods, a judge considering a well-timed objection.

"I have so much to do here, though. I'm pretty swamped."

There is a pause that seems to stretch across the ocean and back. I bite the fever blister on my lip and at the moment it feels really good.

"Carol wants to see Sammy, Dan. It's been over two weeks. Please." He stares at me, blankly. I look over my shoulder and exhale. "I mean, the phone," I say, leaning forward a little. "You haven't answered or returned . . ." He starts blinking like I've just spit in his face. I lean towards him, but just as quickly he composes himself and stands up rigidly. "If there's anything you want to talk—"

He starts to walk away but stops. "That sounds fine," he says. "Sammy should be home in a couple hours. You all can go." He walks up the stairway and I stand there listening. I hear him move from room to room. Then he shuts a door, and there's silence.

I walk through the kitchen and into the study where there are more boxes. Carol's books are still on the shelves. I load them one by one into empty boxes, which I begin to realize—like the others—will never reach Omaha. But I do it anyway. When I've finished, I sit down at Carol's desk and wait for Sammy to come home. There are pictures all over the surface. I don't know how she ever got any work done here. I look over them one by one, the frames organized by color so that they form a spectrum. The pictures are like a storybook: the one of Mom as a teenager performing in a school play that Carol stole from the family album after she died; our father in gigantic glasses, asleep in his office; several of Sammy taken from when he was a newborn up until recently; a series of smiling family vacation shots that make the present all the more surreal, confusing, and sad. And then there's me. I see it in the corner with the black frames. It's my picture from junior year in high school, the one she always threatened to blow up for my fiftieth birthday party. It's from my petulant teenage years, when I'd read a couple of my father's philosophy books and thought I'd figured out the world in its entirety. I'd spend nights locked away in my bedroom with my head in a book, coming out only to debate what I'd read with my father. Things would get pretty heated between us, but I think he was secretly proud. In some sort of bizarre homage to Foucault I shaved my head completely bald. God, that Gorbachevian birthmark I never knew about on the side of my head, purple and slug-like. Of course, I hadn't accounted for the fact that none of my schoolmates knew who Foucault was, and accordingly the first thing they said was that I looked like Telly Savalas. I quickly developed the nickname Kojak, which would haunt me up until graduation, long after my hair had grown back.

She's writing on the legal pad when I walk in holding hands with Sammy later that night. She has on a sweatshirt with the hood pulled tight to her head so she looks like a cosmonaut. Turning the pad over, she reaches out her arm. Everything is in slow motion now, the opening of her eyes, the start of speech, the materialization of a smile. Sammy runs to her bed and she leans forward as much as she can to embrace him. I walk over and kiss her cheek.

"Where's Daddy?" she says.

"Dan had to stay in Lawrence," I say. "Work."

"Right," she says. I try to say something else, but she cuts me off: "Is that a cheeseburger in your hand, or are you just happy to see me?"

I hold up the bag and give her one. "We stopped on the way. Figured you probably hadn't had a burger in a while."

"Contraband," she says. "You're a saint. I've forgotten what they taste like."

"Me too, Nuncle," says Sammy, holding out his hands.

She peels back the wrapper as I sit down in a chair and begin to eat. After I take the first bite, I see Carol just staring at the burger. She sees me watching and takes a small bite. Sammy finishes quickly, and I try to pace myself, but when I finally finish twenty minutes later she is only halfway through. She begins to cough. It's something she's developed recently, these coughing attacks. It goes on for a minute or so, and Sammy and I have to watch her writhe around in bed, helpless. Imagine the worst case of emphysema and double it. She comes out of it disoriented, eyes watery, like someone shaken from dream.

"Hairball?" I venture, and for the first time in a while I say something that makes her laugh.

I turn on the television and Sammy scans the channels until he finds a cartoon, eventually falling asleep at Carol's side. She tells me stories of friends who have made the drive to visit and laughs with futility about the treatments she continues to endure. "They won't let me shave my legs because my skin's so fragile," she says, running a hand over the few patches of hair still left on her head. "So I'm all Euro now. At least they could zap my legs, too."

"What do you say Sammy and I stay with you tonight?"

"He looks comfortable," she says. "I'd like that."

It's late now and the nurse comes in, for the last time we hope. She doesn't put up much fuss about Sammy and me staying. There seems to be a general feeling at this point that there will be no great reversal, no turn for the better, so this small transgression is permissible. She does insist though that Carol get some sleep and we nod our heads like good little children, then Carol flips her the bird when she turns around. "They can't wait until I'm gone. Real estate's profitable here." Her middle finger is long and thinned to the bone. She points it at me: "E.T. phone home."

I flip around the channels until we come upon an old Bogart movie. One with him and Lauren Bacall. It's the one where he's an escaped convict and you don't see his face for the first half of the movie, until his plastic surgery has healed. She's an artist and falls in love with him. When he begins to pull off his mummy-like bandages, Carol turns to me and asks if I'll cut her hair. "I look like a psycho this way. At first I kind of dug the mongoloid look, but I'm just disturbing people now."

"I thought they wouldn't let you, skin's too delicate."

"We won't use a razor blade. Electric," she says, pointing to the table against the wall.

I help her out of bed and into a chair on the far side of the room. The absence of her breast is more noticeable when she stands up, making her look lopsided, like halves of different bodies stitched together. She looks at her chest. "I call it the green-eyed monster."

"Poor Othello," I say, happy anytime I get one of her allusions.

I plug in the electric razor and click it on and off a few times so it sounds like I'm revving an engine. And then I move slowly towards her, humming the theme from Jaws.

"Get over yourself," she laughs.

I stand behind her, tilting her head forward a little. When we were young our mother would cut our hair. She'd lay newspaper all over the kitchen floor and Carol, the oldest, always went first. I'd sit on the counter, watching, and Mom would stand behind her and say in her best Mae West, "Well, should I take it all off, dear?" Carol doesn't respond when I say it now. Her skull is so dry in places it flakes to the touch. Her head seems as fragile as a newborn's, so I hold my breath when I lower the clippers to her head. I have the urge to keep the hair that falls to her shoulder and off the chair, but I'll wait until she falls asleep. When I click the razor off, she sits there a few seconds, running her hand over her head. "Now I look like you, Kojak."

"Hey, who loves you, baby?"

She laughs again and I feel like I'm on a roll.

I help her back to bed, moving Sammy over just a little, and we sit there talking, but not having the talk I expect to have. Not the one about Dan and why he can't bear to visit anymore, or the one where I ask her what she wants me to tell Sammy about her after she's gone. Instead, she asks me about my teaching, how it's going now. I tell her it's going well, that they don't walk all over me anymore. She asks how. "I began starting each day with a joke," I say. "Not my own."

"Thank God," she interjects.

"One of theirs. I let them choose as long as it's clean. They're really into it. They actually want to come to class now, if only for the jokes."

At that she smiles.

We fall asleep with the television crackling. I prop my legs up on one chair and lie back in another for what I know will be the most uncomfortable night of sleep I've ever had. Later that night I wake up when I hear her put the guard down on the side of her bed. I ask what she's doing. "I'm not using that thing with Sammy here," she whispers, pointing to the bedpan. She doesn't want my help. She pauses a moment with her slippered feet hovering lightly above the floor, like they're trying to decide if this will really work, this walking business. Then with one push from her arms, an exertion that seems to exhaust all the strength she has left, she wills herself up, letting out a big bassy fart that sounds something like a conch blown at the start of a tribal ceremony. "Woops," she says, inching along. She stops a moment, thinking. "Are these, I pray you, wind instruments?" I look at her, confused, not getting the reference yet. "And the general so likes your music that he desires you, for love's sake, to make no more noise with it." I think a moment and then I guess.

"Hamlet?"

"Othello," she calls over her shoulder as she slugs into the bathroom. "The kids love that one," she says as the door closes. "Fart jokes and all."

I get the call when I'm in class. It's Dan. He says she's gone. For a moment I think she has snuck out of the hospital, and I imagine her driving down the highway in a convertible. But I know what he means. Arrangements for a service have already been made, as per Carol's instructions. She left Dan a list of how she wanted it done. He reads it to me: an all-purpose wake/visitation/hootenanny, followed by cremation, and the scattering of her ashes sometime later. I can't say anything beyond "Uh huh," as my mind unspools a movie reel of miniature pictures from the past.

It's one of those weird sunny winter days when I drive to Lawrence. Everything seems to be leaking, the whole town melting. All along the highway the frozen tree limbs drip, the sunlight refracts off the ice, and it's blinding. The turnout for Carol's big send-off is larger than I expect. Students, friends, family, colleagues. Our father is too ill to come. Besides, he can't really process it. I tried telling him what happened, but he just kept saying, "Carol? When's she coming to visit?"

We all march out of the cold and into the funeral home, cheeks rosy as porcelain dolls. There is a horribly long series of greetings, forced smiles, hushed sobs, uncomfortable silences, and alarming outbursts. I hear the ineffability of grief expressed in the sound the bodies of two women make who haven't seen each other since they were bridesmaids at Carol's wedding. After I've looked into the eyes of every person and said, "It's okay, thank you for being here," I sit in one of the metal fold-out chairs with Sammy on my lap. Dan kneels before her casket for a long time, alone, his lips moving, trying to explain himself, I imagine. A few lingerers come over to talk while Sammy and I smile as much as we can. When we're alone I ask him how George is doing, and he says he didn't want to come today.

When they bring out the food and wine, people begin to loosen up. Music starts to play, all songs that Carol chose, upbeat stuff: the Beatles and Beach Boys, and later Blondie and *Some Girls*–era Stones. The pall lifts a little, people tell stories, some even dance, and *now* I know it's as Carol imagined it.

———

Sammy spots the package in the bushes by my doorstep when we come home from a movie. He's been spending a lot of time with me. Dan's sister has come to stay with him for a while, helping him to get things back together, and he's agreed to let Sammy stay with me on the weekends. The box is from the hospital in Omaha. I set it in my bedroom and fix Sammy dinner. Later, after he falls asleep, I return to the box with a knife from the kitchen and go to work on the inordinately strong tape job. I lift off the lid and inside are Carol's effects from her room. She must have had them sent to me. I comb over her things: her Dante and Shakespeare, the electric razor, two hats, and a dozen or so pictures. Then I see it, the yellow legal pad. For a moment I wonder if I should read it, but when curiosity gets the best of me and I turn it over I realize she's gotten the last laugh. There are five full pages consisting entirely of titles she'd considered for her autobiography—lines from Shakespeare, from the tragic soliloquies—and they're all crossed out. The script of the final title, the one she appears to have decided on, is so shaky that it looks like it was written by someone with Parkinson's. But it's there, unmistakable, something of her own, for her story: The Cure for Cancer. I grin, studying every curve of the letters. This title seems more appropriate than the Shakespeare—nothing bitter, no "As Flies to Wanton Boys" or "Too Too Sullied Flesh." *Carol*, I think, flipping through the pages.

I put the notepad down and go back to the living room, where Sammy is asleep on the couch. With him coming to stay, I've been forced to unpack and furnish the place finally. I sit on the floor, leaning back close to him, and turn on the television, flipping to the old movie channel, where I watch one I've never seen before. I tilt back my head, thinking about tomorrow when Dan, Sammy, and I will board a plane, heading to scatter Carol's ashes in the ocean off the coast of Maine, where our parents used to take us every summer as children. I imagine her ashes skimming the surface, following the tide out towards the horizon, before sinking to the bottom and becoming coral, like something from *The Tempest*. And with sleep coming on I can feel Sammy's warm breath against my neck, pulling me into dream.

The Antichrist Chronicles

IN THE MONTHS before the lake disappeared, I began having lunch every day with my high school guidance counselor. It was early in the semester, a few weeks into my final year of high school, and I'd taken to eating my lunches with her because Joby had a different lunch period. The counselor's name was Susan and she had the undeserved surname of Cox. It was a name for pranking and practical jokes, a name to be yelled over the intercom by juvenile delinquents during the pledge of allegiance, as Robbie Toobler did the previous spring: *Ms. Cox I need your help! I think I'm in love with you! Ms. Cox aaahhhh* . . . We became friendly after I mistakenly barged into her office looking for the school nurse and stayed for an hour, talking right through fourth-period trig. She must have realized when she didn't recognize me that I had to be a slacker of astronomical proportions, one of the faceless teenage preterite, destined for a life mopping floors at Dillons. And perhaps because of this, she seemed to let her guard down in front of me so that we spoke less as student and counselor than as neighbors on barstools.

That day, the day Joby first started suspecting her father of following her, Susan and I were talking about Mr. Hudson, the seventh-grade English teacher who'd hanged himself earlier in the week. Susan was spending a lot of time at the junior high helping out. Underequipped to handle the aftermath, the principal called for reinforcements, and in Susan he found the right person. Tragedy and general ill fortune were her bread and butter. She was three times a divorcee and her daughter, Jeanie, had a prosthetic leg from the time a doctor's knife slipped during surgery and severed a nerve he was trying to spare. When I asked how she helped the shaken students, she replied, "I don't hold their hands," steeled by her scientist's sense of sympathy. "I listen. Best thing you can do. How can you ever try to reason something like this to kids?" I nodded as the memories of Mr. Hudson slowly stretched back to life inside my head. I'd had him in eighth grade for a month before I was pulled out and switched to the remedial English class. Thinking of him after he was gone, I remembered all sorts of things I hadn't for years, all the thought matter which lies dormant until someone has taken his life: how he was always reading in his classroom after school let out; the way he encouraged his students to call him Jim; his gait, the somber milling of a dreamer. She shook her head and nibbled on the small block of cheese that, along with a Granny Smith apple, she ate every day for lunch. "Still, it's sad, you know. All those kids, most of them dealing with death for the first time. You should see them, Tom. They walk around the hallways like ghosts."

"Like ghosts," I said, wondering what I must have looked like myself walking down the hallway, eyes down, trying to survive those terrifying five minutes of anarchy between bells unmolested as the gauntlet of high-fives and ball-grabbing swallowed up those around me.

Just then there was a knock on the door and Joby popped her head in.

"Hey," she said. She had that look about her, up to no good. "Let's get out of here." Like junkies sick for truancy, we'd developed a bad habit and being so early in the school year we were cutting with a frightening regularity.

I looked at Susan and she threw her hands up. "I don't want to know anything about it."

And with that Joby and I took off down the hallway, ducking out a side door, skulking past Mr. Mineo, the ever watchful parking attendant, and dove into her car, where we both crouched for a few seconds. We waited until he circled around to the other side of the parking lot and then left. When we reached the street and zoomed away from the school, we shouted triumphantly, extending our middle fingers out the window, and Joby turned the music up full blast. She had on a tight red shirt purchased on a recent trip to Kansas City. It was made to look older and less expensive than it was, projecting a silhouette of Lenin flanked by the hammer and sickle. Her finger- and toenails were painted black and she'd drawn little anarchy signs on the white tips of her black Chuck Taylors. "Fascists," she said, looking at our school shrinking in the rearview. Joby spoke in the language of one stuck in permanent revolution. When asked, she'd identify herself as a socialist, but as far as I could tell her platform was a hodgepodge of leftist ideas designed to get a rise out of anyone over the age of thirty. I lacked her passion. Apathy was the bedrock of my ideology, a veritable third rail. Despite this, we'd become friends through high school's strange process of natural selection. Physically we were opposites, too. She was tall and bone-thin, pretty even, with straight brown hair and a long angular face—intimidated the hell out of most boys—and I was short, a little pudgy, invisible but for my big-ass head. We were, Susan liked to tell me, quite the pair.

Joby sped through town, headed for her family's house. Her folks were loaded, a fact she resented more than anything else, the unwashable stink of her own privilege. She lectured constantly about the evils of capitalism, yet drove the SUV her parents gave her for her sixteenth birthday with no sense of irony, with reckless abandon.

The house was part of a private development that bordered the lake that would disappear in a matter of months. We often went to the lake on these afternoons, to smoke-up or talk, taking refuge from our families and school, though today we found ourselves just wandering through the house, looking for anything to distract us. I followed behind her, looking at the back of her Converse, where she had scratched off the All Star and written Anarchy in black marker. Aimlessly, we went from room to room picking things up—home-decorative magazines, antique clocks and wooden pieces, pillows embroidered with passages from the Bible—sometimes commenting on them before setting them back down.

"Where are your parents?" I asked as we stood before the closed door of her father's office, a room I'd never been inside.

"They're out. Mom's garden club meets all afternoon and you know my dad," she said, touching the knob of the door hesitantly.

What she meant was that her dad was rarely home anymore. In fact, beyond a few pictures on the walls, I'd never actually seen him. Apparently he once owned a small livestock farm outside of town and made a fortune selling the sperm of a prize bull. As Joby told it, coming into all this money was a sign, so he sold the farm and moved his family here, where, Born Again, he took up the cause of a church of growing notoriety. He spent most of his time and disposable income developing an ongoing series of videotapes called the Antichrist Chronicles, which he sent to people randomly selected from the phonebook—the "chosen," as Joby referred to them. The intention of the tapes was to show us the myriad ways we had failed God in hopes we'd hightail it for church. Judging from booming attendance rolls and the increasing number of highway billboards that read HELL IS REAL and REPENT AND BE SAVED, the operation was a rousing success.

I was curious. I'd never seen one of the videos before, so when I asked to it seemed to give the afternoon a purpose. Joby eased open the door, slipping inside, and quickly shut it. When she appeared again, she was holding a videocassette. We went down the hallway to the TV room, where I plopped into one of the beanbag chairs.

"This'll be on volume thirteen but it's not edited yet," she said, loading the tape into the VCR. "He's going to start transferring them to DVD soon. Keep up with the technology, you know." She punched a button on the remote and the unsteady picture spilled over the television. We sat quietly as the camera zoomed in on a man bent over a moped chained to a parking meter. I wasn't sure what to make of it until he removed the gas cap and shoved his nose deep into the hole. He huffed the fumes for a good thirty seconds before his legs gave out and he fell to the sidewalk.

"Your dad filmed this?"

"I don't know, maybe. Could be any whacko from his church."

"Do they just wait around for stuff like this to happen?"

"Pretty much," she said, hitting the pause button, which froze on a close-up of the man's face. He looked, I noted, happy.

"I guess that's sort of their point, right?"

"Whatever. Bunch of loons, if you ask me. Sometimes I swear he's following me with that fucking camera. Seriously, no joke." She hit the eject button. "This is creeping me out. Let's go to the lake."

The town where we lived was a small agrarian community in central Kansas, not far from Salina. "The Center of the Center of America," as the welcoming billboard on the edge of town announced. In recent years most of the small, independent farms had gone bust or been swallowed up by corporations and developers. Or worse, they were given small governmental subsidies *not* to farm their land. No one could really make a living on the subsidies so most had foreclosed or turned to agritourism to stay afloat. This was what accounted for our amazing number of pumpkin shooting ranges, shitty Kansan vineyards, country hayrides, and corn mazes in the shape of famous Kansans like Eisenhower and Amelia Earhart. All to avoid foreclosing or watching their tenable land waste away unused, though sometimes even this was not enough, a reality which had given birth to our other great industry: the production and consumption of crystal meth. This was rural Kansas, where Mom-and-Pop farms were giving way to Mom-and-Pop methamphetamine labs. Where the divide between rich and poor was a gulf and with few exceptions like Joby's neighborhood, the streets were lined with doublewides and the cheap bourbon flowed like water. This was a town where everyone knew each other, but no one wanted to admit it.

My dad and I both worked on the weekends. On Saturdays we'd head out early to grab a bite at Ma's diner before the rush and afterwards he'd drop me off at Dillons, where I'd spend six hours mopping floors and bagging groceries, while he went on to his job at Alive With History! The crown jewel of our agritourism boom, Alive With History!—part museum, part amusement park—was comprised of a series of historically recreated farms from different time periods that together told the history of midwestern agriculture on nearly six hundred acres of land. My dad was a "historic actor," which meant he pretended to farm and delivered a spiel on farming techniques of the period whenever a tour group arrived. When the park opened, he started out on the 1785 farm, and every few years moved up to the next, the "Bleeding Kansas" 1859 farm, the post–Civil War 1870 farm, and now had made it to the early modern 1921 farm. For fear of sinking further into the dross of the uncool, I'd never told anyone this, even Joby.

After my shift at Dillons I usually walked over to Sunflower's, where Joby worked as a line cook. I sat at the bar sipping pop, waiting until she finished. It was an awful place, an unfortunate knockoff of Hooters that not so cleverly punned on our state flower, but Joby didn't seem to mind it much. The monstrous sign outside depicted a buxom blonde with triple-D sunflowers for breasts. Today I was seated next to a couple from the northeast who, I gathered from eavesdropping, were driving to California and had mistakenly come in looking for local color, not realizing it was a boobs-and-wings joint. They were staring anxiously at the menu when Joby tapped on my shoulder. A white apron, mottled by sauce and grease stains, hung from her neck. The woman next to me scoffed to her female partner, "Look, they actually have salads in Kansas."

Joby leaned over, an inch away from the woman's ear. She said, "Yes we do, but we smother them in gravy," and walked off.

I followed her out back and she lit a joint by the Dumpster. "All through?" I asked, and she nodded, balling up her apron and dropping it to the ground. We were exhaling little plumes when Jonas walked outside from the kitchen with a bag of garbage. He bussed tables there and occasionally attended our school, but he'd been suspended so many times it was hard to tell if he was actually enrolled anymore. Every month or so, just when I thought he'd surely been expelled, I'd see him walking the hallways or sleeping on his desk in class.

"Hey," he said, looking at Joby. "What're you doing?"

"Nothing," Joby said. "Gonna walk around or something."

Jonas had shaved his hair into a Mohawk, though the remaining swatch was trimmed so close that it looked less punk than military.

He laughed and put up his hands. "Sorry, didn't mean to interrupt any-thing." He was almost a foot taller than me, but I wanted so badly then to bruise him in the shins.

"Fuck off, Jonas," Joby sighed languidly, like the chorus of a sultry song about a never-ending summer. Our friendship had always been asexual, something that seemed to confuse those around us. "Come with."

Smoking the joint put us in a mood to walk around, so there the three of us were, watching the lights from the bars and pool halls switch on. Neon bands of light snaked through the dark and the smell of ozone singed the air. Men in newly bought cowboy hats practiced their strut around town, wearing multiple turquoise rings and belt buckles the size of championship boxing titles. It had been a brutal summer, the heat unyielding, and even now in mid-September we wondered when it would cool. The landscape was dominated by long stretches of sunflow-ers that would only disappear when the heat broke. We walked through town saying things like, "It's too hot to smoke," but did so anyway.

Paranoia was a major buzz kill with the local ragweed we smoked, and later when it was full dark Joby said again that she thought her father was following her. She was convinced he had started planting microphones and miniature cameras in her clothes. "That's the kind of shit they do in totalitarian regimes," she said, her eyes wild. I tried to calm her, but she wouldn't settle down. When we got back to the parking lot, Jonas wiped his nose on his shirtsleeve and held out his hand. "Wanna try? Won't make you paranoid as weed." In his palm sat an 8-ball of the icelike chips that had provoked the President's drug czar to compare what was happening in rural parts of Kansas and Mis-souri to the crack epidemic that plagued inner cities in the '80s. Joby was looking down the neck of her shirt, trying to find some means of surveillance, and only looked at Jonas's hand after having found none, relieved. "I think I'm clean."

When I was three, my mother came home from work, fixed my father dinner, and put me to bed. Then, that night, after my dad had fallen asleep in front of a *Star Trek* rerun, she packed a bag, left the house, and disappeared. I say disappeared because there was never a note or phone call, never a reason or explanation, just the reality: she was gone, vanished. I knew all of this only from the bits I'd been able to pull out of my father when he'd had a few drinks. Without one he'd tell me I was adopted. There were no pictures. All evidence of her existence was gone. I remembered so little, a voice mostly. We'd lived in Kansas City then, where my dad was a Lit professor at UMKC, but after she left he moved here to get himself together. His uncle Mort owned a little bar in town and we stayed with him a while. Dad spent most of his days drinking at the bar, which is how he developed his habit. For a large part of my youth he collected unemployment and lived off savings. When uncle Mort died, my dad sold the bar and only began working at Alive With History! when the money was nearly gone. The only traces of his former life as an impassioned lecturer of poetry survived in fragments, popping up unexpectedly, as in notes he'd leave on the kitchen counter: *This is just to say: I've ventured to the store. Shall return henceforth, joyously, Redcrosse.*

It was several Saturdays later, in early November, that the lake disappeared. From our table at Ma's diner my dad rattled the newspaper. "You'll never believe what happened." I was looking down at my plate, trying to discern whether the black flakes floating in my yolk were cigarette ash or pepper, and mumbled back, asking what's up. When he didn't respond, I looked at him. His mammoth eyebrows dwarfed his eyes, and he'd long since stopped trying to control the Einsteinian flair of his wild gray hair. He was wearing a black t-shirt with a picture of Leonard Nimoy under the heading *What Would Spock Do?* and he was grinning, holding the front page of the paper for me to see. As the wave of intrigue moved across his face, he looked like a mad scientist from some old Universal horror film on the brink of major discovery, of something that could either save the world or end everything.

After breakfast we went to see the lake. I studied the article as my father drove uncle Mort's old truck, a big pewter tank of a thing that will survive long after the asteroid hits. I was slow to realize that it was our lake—Joby's and mine, the one by her house—that had vanished. The article said officials weren't sure what had caused the strange occurrence.

"What do you think happened?" my dad said, shaking his head. "What happened to all that water?"

"No idea," I said. I folded up the paper and dropped it into the foot well. "Aliens," I offered, and before I could take it back the word was suctioned from my mouth like a losing lottery ball. He said nothing, but I could feel him bristle at my sarcasm.

My father was a Believer.

We arrived to find a growing crowd of rubbernecks looking at the hole where the lake had been only yesterday. There was a post-Apocalyptic air about the place that seemed to fit with the pre-millennium angst the country was working through. The lakebed was swampy with mud, sailboats stranded in the muck, and dead fish lay decomposing in profile. The stench was awful. The local news media were live on the scene, updating the fact that they had no new information minute by minute. It was dizzying; the headline *Water Stolen!* ran on tickertape around my head. In the distance, all around the perimeter of the hole, were the huge lakefront homes like Joby's and behind them was a new development of condominiums. I studied the crowd but couldn't find her.

"Where the hell did all of it go?" my dad said quietly, with a true sense of awe.

It was hard for me to imagine him in that other life. Some of my earliest memories involved the two of us Dumpster-diving, rummaging through rot and stink, for things people had thrown away—so unwavering was his commitment to avoid work. As scavengers for the debris of other people's lives, we populated our house with their unwanted memories, those possessions whose histories we'd never know. The house was still largely made up of them, even though things were different now. In some ways he was better, and in others he'd never been worse. I knew there were parts of himself he never let me see, parts that were pushing him farther away from reality, deeper into space. I watched him glance over his shoulder as he pulled a silver flask from his pocket. Raising it to his lips, he held it there like a microphone: "Star date: zero, zero, dash, one, nine, nine, nine. We have successfully discovered the site of a failed Klingon attempt to end life as we know it on this strange planet. So much like Earth," he said, then stopped, with a pause that would give Shatner a boner, "but entirely different."

Susan looked at her reflection in the glass that framed a Van Gogh self-portrait, inching close to the painting and pulling down the skin below her eyes so that she looked like a basset hound. "Jesus, I look like hell." She was telling me about the trouble she'd had trying to get her daughter Jeanie's new prosthetic leg; they'd driven to Kansas City three separate times for fittings that failed her five-year-old's stub. There was a picture of Jeanie on her desk, a pretty sprite of a girl with saucers for eyes, blonde hair, and a smile that could have moved millions of boxes of cereal.

Susan's face bore the topography of a hard life. She was pretty, though. Very pretty, in fact. She'd broken the hearts of many high school boys who feigned mental instabilities and interest in college just to sit in her office, so I felt lucky to be whatever it was we were. "Have you thought about schools," she said, picking up the apple on her desk and tossing it to me. She'd been doing this lately, asking me to think about college.

"No," I said, and lobbed it back to her.

"Where do you think you might like to apply?" She underhanded it to me again.

I threw it back. "Did you hear about the lake? It disappeared."

"What part of the country do you think you'd like to be in?"

"They have no idea what caused it."

"There are only two more chances to take the ACT. Have you signed up?"

"Do you believe in aliens? My dad actually thinks they might be mixed up in this."

"It's important you sign up to take the test, Tom."

"My dad says they could have a strong interest in our water supply because of the high iron content."

"Colleges will not accept you if you don't take the test."

"He says there's an outside chance they might give the water back," I said, as Susan caught the apple we'd been tossing back and forth the entire time. "But it's best not to get our hopes up."

"Your father," she said, setting the apple on her desk. "What does a professor think of his son not wanting to attend college?" It caught me a little off guard, this lie. Like everyone else, I'd told her he still taught. I said that he was leaving it up to me and she nodded, eyebrows raised, sighing. She looked at the file on her desk with my name on it and said, "Tell me about your mother."

"I have to go," I said, standing quickly. "Class," I nodded towards the hallway.

She rolled her eyes, saying she needed a cigarette, like it was an invitation or peace offering, but this time I would not follow her outside.

After school Joby and I drove to her house and walked to the lake. There were men wandering around in rubber suits that looked as though they should have been handling plutonium. They were tossing the dead fish into big yellow barrels. The smell was horrible, pestilent, the ground still muddy. There were people walking around the lakebed in fly-fishing boots and, for a reason lost on me, hardhats. They were setting up surveying equipment.

A small group of onlookers still crowded the perimeter and Joby spotted her father amongst them, filming, so we quickly walked the other way, a half-mile on to the abandoned baseball field where a minor league team once played years ago. The advertisements lining the outfield wall were all faded and the field had grown over with dead sunflowers, scrub, and brush. Joby took a can of black spray paint out of her bag and went to the fence, spraying over ads for athlete's foot salve and Simonize, writing little enigmatic anarcho-haikus like *This is Terrorism; Fuck Nazi Sympathy; Anarchism is the Union of Lovers;* and the classic *God is Gay.* Afterwards we walked to home plate, where the grass was thinner, and sat down. She lit a joint, took a couple puffs and passed it to me.

"Out here, everybody's crazy with looking for something," Joby said. "I swear, sometimes I think it's only God or drugs that ever finds them though." She pulled her long brown hair back tight, then let it fall down her shoulders. "Like my dad. He thinks this all has to do with God." She motioned with her chin in the direction of the barren lake as I passed the joint back. "He's been out there every day with his video camera recording what's happening. Gonna put it on one of his stupid tapes." She flicked the ash off the tip of her Converse. "At dinner he talks about how God took the water to punish us for our sins." She laughed sadly, shaking her head. "And people wonder why I'm the way I am. It's like how they say preachers' daughters are the most rebellious, only my dad's not a preacher. He's a psycho."

"My dad didn't do anything but watch *Star Trek* for an entire decade after my mom left. Barely even spoke to me."

We often told stories about our fathers, not in a bid to one-up the other but to commiserate, the hope that in speaking about them we might begin to understand them. That day at the field I remember Joby telling me about her last attempt to reconcile with hers. It was a few years earlier and at her father's urging she'd agreed to go to one of his church's rallies. That night he drove a busload of followers all the way to Lawrence on the night of the big KU-Mizzou basketball game. There were thirty or so others from the church and they congregated in the parking lot outside the Allen Fieldhouse, holding signs and posters, waving them at fans who walked past. "It was right after Oklahoma City and the poster I held had a picture of the Federal Building after the bomb exploded under the heading my father had written in black marker that morning: *God's Wrath for Gays.* Everyone was holding something similar—pictures of the Challenger exploding, of Matthew Shepard, aborted fetuses."

"Jesus."

"Exactly," she said. "I knew then there was no hope for us." She took a last drag and let the nub fall to the dirt. "The thing is, he wasn't always like that. He was once just a cattleman farmer." She put her head down and shook it, then looked up with sudden conviction. "You don't understand. These people aren't harmless, Tom—they elect presidents, for Christ's sake."

Later that night when I arrived back at the house, I found my dad sitting on the couch, dressed up as crewman Scotty from Star Trek. It's important to know this was not abnormal. "There's my boy," he said in a faux Scottish accent that was a conflation of Irish, Australian, and Jamaican. I'd almost forgotten about the convention that weekend in Kansas City. He'd been going to them ever since I could remember and liked to try and get into character a day or two before—he was almost Method about it. I'd heard stories about how he once went to a convention as Uhura, dressed in blackface and drag nonetheless. "That was Toronto '77," he'd blushed. "You could get away with that then. You should have seen it, Tommy—thousands of Canadians saying 'ooter space.'" I could smell the scotch on his breath and saw the tumbler, nearly full, tilting half off a coaster bearing the likeness of George Takei. On the television ran a special about how the 1969 moon landing was faked. This was heresy in my father's house, but he seemed to watch with the interest of an interloper, a sports coach who's snuck into the opposing team's gym to see what plays they're going to run. The TV flashed the familiar pictures of Neil Armstrong beach-balling across the lunar surface with the voiceover: "Notice that the flag isn't moving. Our expert scientists attest that the shadows are reversed from normal—they're *physically* impossible." The screen switched to show a man standing in a NASA-style control room.

My father drained his glass in one throat-searing funnel, then leaned forward and started rocking, trying to get some momentum off the couch. I gave him a little push and he rose, banging his knee against the corner table as he left the room. I turned my attention back to the television, where I learned that the moon landing was actually filmed on a Hollywood soundstage, simply a strategic bluff to scare off the Russians as our countries fought to determine whose galactic balls were bigger. "Interstellar brinksmanship," said the host, grinning with the self-satisfaction of one having his testicles feathered by a quill. "Imagine," he said, slowly raising a hand to the wall of clocks, monitors, and glowing buttons behind him, "the repercussions."

I flipped the channel and caught the tail end of the national news. More about our virtuous bombing of Serbia.

"What are you watching that for?" my dad said when he returned. "Turn it back to my show."

But it was too late; the moon-hoax special was already over and the familiar opening music of our local news had begun. There was a breaking story about the lake. That entire week people had been speculating about what happened, flooding the editorial pages, and to try and quell the fervor the mayor called a press conference. The news anchor explained this as the screen showed the stout mayor trotting out a team of white-coats to address the media. Without wasting a moment, the lead scientist offered a logical, if unusual, explanation for the strange phenomenon: a sinkhole formed when water eroded the limestone deep underground and created pockets in the rock. The entire twenty-three-acre body of water disappeared into one of these sinkholes, worming deep into the ground below town. In what seemed a stab at humor, he grinned, analogizing: "Think of a plug being pulled on a bathtub."

"These guys don't know similes from metaphors, their asses from sinkholes," my father mused, shaking his head.

When the press conference finished, after my dad had had another drink, I helped him upstairs to his room, where he plopped down on the bed.

"Are you drunk?" I asked.

"I am," he grinned, stretching out the declaration, "not."

I sat at the foot of the bed, the only spot free from the piles of creased Sci-fi books littering the surface. Gone were the hardback volumes of modern poetry; my father now taught exclusively from the canon of the mass market paperback.

"Tell me about Mom," I said.

"Nothing to tell. It's just you and me, kid. I grew you in the basement like a sea monkey."

"What happened to her?"

"Moved to Mexico. Joined the circus. CIA. Take your pick."

"Dad!"

He was quiet a minute, eyes closed. He shook his head back and forth and began humming some sort of Irish ballad. Then his eyes opened abruptly. "I am not drunk," he said, raising a single finger. "I'm a romantic. I'm a poet. I am the bard of agriculture!" His voice was strained, and he lowered his hand, accidentally knocking over a stack of books that were at his side. He gave a little shrug, as if to say *That's life*, and turned off the lamp on his bedside table, filling the room with darkness.

With winter's descent, the question dividing most of the town was what to do about the lake. After the geologists and surveyors gave the okay to work, there was still the matter of cost. Because the lake was private property, the subdivision's residents were saddled with the burden of fixing it. Some estimates were as high as $5,000 a household. Factions formed within the subdivision: those who thought the city should assume some of the cost; those who wanted the lake to be filled with dirt and turned into either park or parking lot; people who wished to move; and the few, like Joby's parents, who could afford to pay and were willing to do so, whatever the cost. To further complicate the matter, the cold weather meant that it would be spring before anything could be done about it. The papers covered the drama daily. Even the major circulations in Wichita and Kansas City began carving out space for updates on the lake, for our little town, this theater of the absurd.

Susan and I were sitting in her office discussing the drudgery of the holidays when school resumed after break. We were oathless and irresolute in the New Year, this new millennium. She told me about Jeanie finally getting her new prosthetic, how on the way home from the hospital they composed a new song: *All I Want for Christmas Are My Two Front Feet*. "She's such a good sport about it," she smiled. I told her about how my dad and I settled for watching *It's a Wonderful Life* with gigantic twin mixing bowls of instant mashed potatoes on our laps.

Before the bell rang, she said, "I need some fresh air," meaning she wanted to smoke, so we left. As I followed her down the hallway, a few students looked at us, whispering to one another or laughing. Susan didn't seem to notice and I thought them jealous. Secretly, their jeers made me feel good, chosen. Outside it was cold. I put on my black stocking cap and she pulled up the collar of her coat. She took out a cigarette and rifled through her purse for a lighter. I could make out the callused and yellowing tips of her fingers and suddenly wanted to touch them. Her hair wisped around her face in the wind. Her ears were already red; I offered her my hat, but she declined. "You know," she said, holding a hand to block the wind. "You missed the ACT exam. I checked the roll." She spoke out the side of her mouth. I shook my head. Here we go again, I thought. "If you just take the damn thing you'll at least have some options." I didn't have a good excuse for not taking the test, other than that I didn't want to take the goddamn test. That and because Joby and I had plans for the next year that didn't involve college. "Higher education is indoctrination," Joby liked to say. Relieved of the burdens of schooling, she planned on leading the Revolution from a studio apartment in central Kansas, while I'd be right alongside her, still working at Dillons most likely. Apathy, remember. I'd accepted my lot. I told Susan this and she said, "That's the most bullshit excuse I've ever heard."

A group of kids walked past us. One of them waved at Susan but she didn't see.

"I mean, why do you want me to take the test so bad anyway? What do you care?"

"Because I want you to get the hell out of here!" she said, throwing her hands onto my shoulders. Her outburst took me aback and the commotion caught the attention of the kids, who turned to look at us. Quickly, Susan took her hands away. "You don't want to end up in this place," she shook her head. "You should see what else is out there." She told me there was only one more test next month, the last before applications were due. "Promise you'll take it," she said. I hadn't figured out whether to honor it or not, but I told her I would, and that made her smile.

As with many vices, the beauty and bane of crystal meth is its simplicity. Anyone who has Internet access and the will to shoplift from the drugstore can manufacture it. It was a serious problem in our town. All of a sudden iodine, camphor oil, and cold medicines were flying off the shelves, stuffed in the bottoms of lint-filled pockets and the crotches of unchanged underwear. Those with more gumption stole the anhydrous ammonia tanks from farms. And it wasn't just the poor and desperate who were making it. People were paying their mortgages, financing their farms, and saving for college funds and retirement. It was making fortunes for suppliers and taking the hair and teeth of the addicted. I knew all of this and yet Joby's habit happened right underneath my nose.

One night late in spring, when the weather had finally started to warm, Joby invited some people over to her house. Her father was out of town for the weekend at a religious convention in Kansas City and her mom, silently sympathetic to Joby's misery, agreed to host a party, this anti-prom. Joby invited about twenty or so of us, including Jonas, and her mom greeted us at the door with an uncertain smile, a look that seemed to say *Don't trample my flowerbeds and please use coasters.* Inside, cold 30-packs of beer were stacked like bullion. People were talking, playing music they were too cool to dance to, and trying to find a vacant closet to fondle one another in. Joby wore a red shirt with Che Guevara emblazoned on it and she'd paid a salon to put her hair in dreadlocks. Later, when most people had passed out or fallen asleep, Joby told me to follow her. We were both pretty soused by then and she pulled me by the hand to her dad's study. It was the first time I'd been inside. There were several bookshelves lined with videocassettes flanking both sides of a messy desk.

"Check it out," she said, pointing at the bookshelf by the door. "They're of the lake." I looked closer and saw they were dated consecutively.

"He's been filming every day since it disappeared?"

"We can watch if you want," she said. For a long minute we were quiet and then she moved closer to me, within a few inches, and said, "You can stay here tonight, you know." She began rubbing her hands against my chest. This surprised me. I didn't know what to do; I didn't do anything. She rubbed harder, then leaned into me. Still I didn't move. It must have been like hugging a 2x4. I'd had this dream before, where Joby confesses she's really loved me all this time and we make love and live happily ever after, but I was frozen, as though anything I might say or do would make her stop. Then she kissed me, our lips bumping together awkwardly like seventh-grade dance partners. "Do it with me, please. It'll be fun."

"You really want to?" I finally managed to say, eyes still closed.

She leaned closer, laughing a small amorous laugh, and bit the lobe of my left ear. I inhaled the cocoa butter scent of her skin and for a moment it made me feel good, but quickly the smell turned oppressive and I felt trapped.

"I don't have a condom," I said.

I heard her breath catch and she pulled back from my chest, her scent wafting away. When my eyes opened I saw she was holding a small baggie. Quickly, she stuffed the meth back in her pocket and lowered her head, rushing out of the room. I let her go, standing still for a minute, confused, before sneaking out to the deck to get my head together. There I watched the soft glow in the sky that precedes the sun in the early morning. There was just enough light to make the ground visible. I traced the circumference of the empty hole below me. The ground of the lakebed was fully thawed now, deep and cavernous, like the site where a meteor had tried to end the world.

As I leaned my elbows on the wood railing, a flicker of light from the trees caught my eye. I looked below me and saw it again, a glint, like the face of a watch momentarily catching the sun. I squinted. It was still quite dark and I tried to focus my eyes, but I couldn't quite make it out. Then I saw it again, the little flash, several yards away from the first. "Who's there?" I called out. There was no response and all I heard was the sound of something brushing past limb and leaf.

I went inside to find Joby, to tell her that people were prowling around, and when I walked downstairs I had to step over the bodies of sleepers splayed and passed out on the basement floor. Joby and Jonas were sitting on the carpet, backs to the wall. She looked at me, expressionless. Jonas had his arm around her. "Tom, you gotta take a hit off this," he said, holding out a CD case with several thin dust lines on top.

"Don't," Joby said, holding back his arm. "He doesn't have a condom."

The morning after Joby's party I slept through the last ACT exam, and the morning after that the school fired Susan. Joby delivered the news in a note passed during chem. I asked to go to the bathroom and rushed to Susan's office but it was too late; her stuff was already cleared out, as though she'd just up and vanished. Joby arrived a minute later. "I saw her earlier, loading boxes into her car before school." These were the first words she'd spoken to me since the party.

"What'd she say?" I asked, stepping inside the empty office and looking around. "Didn't she say anything?"

"That she was leaving."

"Is that all?"

"No, Tom. She said she loves you."

"Fuck you."

We were both still mad about the other night, but a kindness seemed to come over Joby then. She exhaled heavily. "She said with the school year almost over she was strongly encouraged to leave now and spend the summer looking for other employment because 'her conduct had not been professional.'"

"Professional? What the hell does that mean?"

"You tell me."

I looked sharply at Joby for the first time and then turned my attention back to the vacant room. I wanted to ask if Susan said to tell me anything, then felt stupid and young for thinking she might have. Joby moved closer, touching my shoulder. "Come on, let's cut out." I didn't see Mr. Mineo anywhere when we ran for Joby's car. He'd never missed a day, so far as I could tell, and for a fleeting instant I thought it had to be related to Susan. I pictured the two of them in a car, fleeing this awful place together. Joby said we needed to talk, that she had something to tell me. She asked where I wanted to go. "To the lake?"

"Head for the highway."

She took her foot off the gas and our speed dropped sharply. "I'm not taking you to find her. She's gone. Get over it."

"Just drive," I said.

She eased back onto the accelerator and periodically I gave directions, telling her to switch lanes here, to make a turn there, and soon we were sitting in a parking lot. "Mind if I ask what the hell we're doing at this place?" she said. I told her to follow me. Begrudgingly, she obliged, removing a flaccid cigarette from her jeans as we walked toward admissions. After I paid, we entered into the 1850-style frontier town that served as the gateway to the farms. We passed different trade booths and crafts stores, places where you could watch horses being shoed or glass blown, where you could dip your own votives or mint bronze coins. Joby regarded the people dressed in the oppressive period costumes they'd sweat through all summer, unimpressed. We walked to the south end of the miniature town and caught a tram to the 1921 farm, passing the 1785, 1859, 1870, and 1900 farms in a slow succession of agrarian history.

We exited the tram and walked past a reconstructed farmhouse and paddock to a wooden fence on the edge of a cornfield, where before a crowd of schoolchildren a man leaned against a restored model of one of the first tractors.

He looked tired in his worn brown trousers and heavy boots. He removed his rumpled period hat and wiped his brow, smiling at the kids before him.

"Hot enough for you?"

"I don't understand what we're—look, I have to tell you something, Tom."

"That's my father," I interrupted.

Joby looked confused, turning to study the man with the crazy hair, wielding several stocks of corn. For all the stories we'd shared about our fathers I'd never been honest about this one. Dad saw us and waved before delivering his short monologue on what farming was like in 1921, not long after the world had become modernized. Business industries were creating new innovations that would forever make farming easier and more productive, he told them. What he didn't say was that these were the same innovations and developments that would eventually make it near impossible for family farms to exist today. He seemed at ease, smiling at the kids as he handed each child a cornstalk. "Well, you ain't no use to me standing around like this," he said, assuming a countryish accent. "My wife," he said, motioning toward the white farmhouse, inside of which was a woman who cooked authentic meals for tour groups to sample while delivering her own speech on the woman's role of running of a homestead. "The missus is expectin' corn for supper. I'm runnin' behind today, see, and I need your help. Who here knows how to husk corn?" The kids looked at one another, clueless, and he proceeded to show them, first tearing off the corn from the stalk and slowly folding back the layers of husk to reveal the silk-covered kernels. The kids struggled to do the same, looking surprised when they unearthed the yellow vegetable. My father smiled as he walked up and down the line, offering encouragement, so comfortable talking to them. He looked amazingly functional, as he often did despite the disease. Without nerves or edge, this must have been what it was like all those years ago teaching students at the university.

When it was over, my father momentarily broke character, unable to resist telling the children to live long and prosper, and Joby and I walked away.

"Why did you bring me here?" she asked.

"Don't know," I said, mumbling something about truth.

She didn't ask me why I lied to her about my dad, perhaps because she didn't have to; she must have known we tend to believe what we need to.

As we walked back to the tram and through the town to the parking lot, Joby revealed her own secret. She told me that she applied to UMKC in the fall, just to keep her options open, though she never mentioned it to me. She was sorry, but she'd been accepted and was going. I watched our feet move as we walked in a strange syncopated rhythm. "Aren't you going to say anything?" she asked. I thought of a story

Susan once told me about how Jeanie sometimes still felt the leg that was gone—that when Susan got her ready for bed Jeanie would take off her prosthetic and point to the air below her kneecap, saying, "My leg hurts, Mommy. Will you rub it?"

"You need to quit that junk, you know," I said. "It'll ruin you good."

She didn't respond, didn't say anything until we got to her car, asking if I needed a ride. I told her I was going to wait for my dad's shift to finish, that it was almost over. We both seemed to sense the finality—that whatever connection we'd had would never be the same—and understood the lack of fanfare with which it arrived.

After she pulled out of the parking lot, I noticed the headlights of a black SUV, identical to Joby's, turn on. The light shining right at me, I couldn't make out the driver but had the feeling I knew who it was. It was a cool evening. Small buds from a flowering tree floated in clusters through the air, and for a second it seemed that if I were just waking up now I might think it was snowing. I stood there looking at him, a silhouette in a hulking car, knowing I was being filmed, and stretched my arms out.

We are all reversed in some ways, our lives shading backwards like the shadows on the moon. We're fed-up and off-kilter, a little crazy or too spacey, poisoned by the lake water in our soil and drugs sprung from our towns, and yet we find ways to inch forward despite our best efforts not to. And so, soon began the summer, my first as high school graduate. These were the three months I found myself still pushing mop and broom over the floors of Dillons, whispering for customers to watch their step when someone accidentally dropped a bottle of wine or juice, setting up my yellow cautionary signs and moving the wet mop head in circles, watching the maroon stain spread and dilute, as though something—some sign—might reveal itself in the mess. This was the summer I wrote long letters to Joby that came back unanswered in envelopes stuffed with pamphlets requesting donations for the Zapatistas, Amnesty International, and Serbian civilians who'd lost limbs in the NATO bombing. This was when my dad and I went to see the lake every week, watching as they slowly refilled it with water; a time when I'd finally open the brochures of nearby community colleges to see what they offered. This was the summer I was so alone I could barely stand it, thinking of Susan and Jeanie, Joby, my mother—all those women— imagining where they might be, what they were doing. And though I knew that if I didn't leave soon the town would swallow me forever, I hated myself for not having been able to. This was the summer I returned home from work each day hoping to find a videocassette lodged in the mailbox, a tape we could watch, that would reveal all our sins and transgressions, so that then we might finally be free from them.

Silver Creek, 1969

DO YOU REMEMBER? Do you remember that barn, Colton? Silver Creek. And that man, the big one, who got me. We'd hid inside his drafty barn for three days, cheeks pressed hard to the slats, hoping he wouldn't find us. Damn, these years. The tortures of a long memory are endless hours to think back on it all, wondering where you are now. Remember how we started out? Two lost souls with no jobs, telling tales, saucing it up in the cheapest bar in Kansas City, Kansas. You said hey to me that first night and we talked for the entire evening. "Colton Bunce," you said, extending your hand and me mine. "Where'd you get a name like that?" I asked and, like you'd answered it a million times already, you said, "southeast Missouri," which made us both laugh. But when we saw each other the next day, at bar's open, our eyes met with mutual embarrassment and shame. The things we told each other the night before about jobs, successful careers, and loving wives were lies and it was clear that all we really were was two louts, sick for the drink. But instead of turning around to leave, pretending you didn't see me, and hoping we never crossed paths again, you came in and slapped me on the back, "How's work going, buddy?" And I said, "Step into my office. Got a meeting with the boss here in a few minutes. Not looking forward to it—asshole's tighter than a snare drum." You laughed and then me too, and you said, "Screw your boss. Have a drink with me." We spent all afternoon in the bourbon, talking or not talking, so it went.

"So, no family then?" you said later after a stretch of silence, and I nodded. "Was married once years ago, until she up and left. When she actually got to know me," I winked. "Know what I mean?" Right then you exhaled in that way you used to—two quick snorts through the nostrils, like an antsy horse. "And you," I smiled, "tell me when you lost yours." You let one half of your face grin and said, "No lies. Got a wife, sad to say. She don't speak to me none, but . . . And a boy," you added, nodding. "But soon he's off to fight." You set down your glass and nodded at the bartender. "The war," I said and you said, "Yeah, the war."

It wasn't until your boy shipped out, two months later, that we did, too. Left the city in my beaten old Ford. Your wife had had it, kicked you clean out. You said California, that that was where your boy would be coming back in two years, but I figured we'd be lucky if the jalopy saw us to Denver. We made it maybe two hundred miles out before she gave up on us, somewhere we'd never heard of, the kind of place that didn't exist until you were stuck there. Do you remember? You spent a good while under the shade of the propped hood, huffing, pretending like you knew what the hell you were doing. I sat on the trunk and watched the cars speed past, listening to you mumble about the engine. "Let's leave her," I finally said, walking up to the front of the car. "We'll walk—catch a ride. Hitch. Hell, we've got two years to get to California," I laughed. Your head was hovering over the steamy insides, hands smudged black with grease. "We can at least scrap it and make a few bucks," you said, and you were right. We found a man who ran a garage and wrecker service a couple miles down who said it was undrivable but gave us twenty dollars for parts—some kind of kindness, I suppose. And that moment, after getting the money from that man, we both had the same kind of notion, which is to say we were ready to get nice and drunk. The man with his hard little eyes pointed us in the direction of a place. I still remember the name—the Den. It made our old spot in the city look classy. It was the sort of place we might have fit in well if you could have kept your mouth shut. It was only the early afternoon but we faced several backsides lining bar stools as we walked through the door. I later gathered that they'd all been let off from the tire factory that had all but closed. We strode up and sat on two seats in the corner. "Two Millers," you said in a snappy city way and the stubbly fat man just looked at the television—more on about the moon, still, months later—scratching once at his neck. "This moon business is fascinating, Chubbs, but we got a new ball team in Kansas City. How about putting on the game." The fat man's fingers slowed their scratching and he finally looked over at us, as did the row of eyes to our left. I know you remember this part, though, because they were smart and waited until we were liquored up before beating the piss out of us. The fat man and his friends stood over us, and after everyone had gotten in their licks, he searched our pockets and took the last of our money.

I swear we must have walked for thirty hours before finding Silver Creek, feeling our bodies expand and shape around our new bruises. In the early fall the cool air siphoned into our arms and chests through the holes in our jackets, filling us with sickness and hurt. The crushing silence of that long walk. Do you remember how you said, "Just for the night" when we arrived at dusk that first evening, unaware how things'd shake out. How relieved we were then as we watched the house and farm from a ditch for a good half hour, seeing the man and woman sit down for dinner, to make sure we knew everyone was inside the house before slipping into the barn. It was cool in there. A stable barn smelling of stool, we moved past the itchy horses and blank-faced cows, through the stink and mess, to the back where there were sacks of feed and bales of hay. There we shoved a couple together and slid behind them, pulling our coats over us, and slept for hours that felt like days.

I woke sometime in the predawn and watched you sleep for a while, the way your chest lowered and raised, lowered and raised, like you were running somewhere mighty fierce. Then I heard something. The door began to open and you startled. I set my hand on your chest and a finger before my nose, telling you to hush quiet. A man entered the barn, moving amongst the stables. He was heavy and breathing hard, his mind set on something alright. He came over by us and grabbed a sack of feed. I swear my heart nearly leapt out my throat, but the big man must not have seen the tips of our shoes poking out from behind the bales. When he left, you were all worked up, ready to head on. "Can't go to jail," you panicked, but I said we should stay for a while, rest up a few days, that we could live off what we could scrounge and sleep in the barn. I told you we should study the big man's routine so he wouldn't catch us. He'd never know. "What about drink?" you said. "This place is called Silver Creek," I said, pointing to the door, where it was painted in black letters. "There's bound to be a creek around here where we can get water." But I realized what you were really asking when you repeated, a little lower, "But what are we going to do about the drink?"

You nearly shook yourself to death that first night, less from the night chill than the horrible ache. I was feeling the pains, too, but not near as bad. After our close call with the big man I decided on a new spot in the barn behind some bins in the loft. I watched you shiver and mumble, placing my coat over you, and leaned back against a crate. The next morning by the time the man had come and gone, sacks of feed in each hand, herding the animals out, you were nearly out of your head with the shakes. You said the damnedest things, stranger than if you were lost in the sauce even. Stuff I imagine you wanted nobody to ever hear—about your wife and your boy. Always your boy. That's how I learned his name, Scott. That's how I learned the one true thing about him. I never got that bad, though my fingers ached so much I wished they'd just go on and fall off already. I took care of us for a while when you were lowly in that way. You slept and shook for another day and after watching the big man's movements, I ran out one night looking for the creek but never found it, so I was bold enough to sneak up close to the house and use the hose to fill a pail I borrowed from an old dray horse, who just looked at me, snorted. Stole some feed, too. Bone meal though, same as you'd use for fertilizer, which is my way of saying it tasted of shit. Quarry-hard as it was, it nearly broke my teeth. I tried to get you to nibble on it once or twice, but you spit out the bits I put in your mouth. "That's not what I need," you said, shaking still, teeth like hooves on cobblestone. "The other stuff. Just enough to get us out

of here, back to a main road. We'll hitch a ride from there." Your eyes
were small and desperate, trying to hold on, like the dying embers of a
gone fire. "To California," you said before falling back into that other
world, mumbling.

I cupped some water in my hand and dripped a little in your mouth,
running the coolness over your gums before slipping out into the dark.
I'd seen the previous night that the lights in the house had shut off
right near full dark. The knob on the doorway to the kitchen eased
with only the slightest squeak, and then I was inside, moving across
the floor, not much quicker than a snail's fastest. I was sure any second the man was gonna appear or call the cops on us, on me. I paused
after every step, listening for anything. The house buzzed loudly with
its own kind of silence. When I finally found what must have been the
only bottle of liquor in the house, a liter of no-name hooch in a cabinet
above the stove, I couldn't resist taking a sniff right there. Nothing in
that life ever tasted so good, I swear. I knew this is what you'd need to
put in your mouth and be your old self again. I was too eager, though,
and bumped the leg of a chair that knocked against the table, groan-
ing a bit. I froze, hearing a creak upstairs. But then there was nothing, so I moved on out quickly. The dry splintery grass crackled with
each step and I hurried, imagining your expression when you saw the
bottle. Damned if I wasn't almost there when the big man caught me in
the shoulder from the doorway. First, only like a horsefly stinging, but
then my arm was powerless and I watched the bottle fall from my hand,
thudding into a patch of dirt where the grass had been kicked up. And
then I was there on the ground, reaching out for it. I didn't even realize,
feeling the warmth soak my shirt, thinking the bottle must have broke
and run onto me and how much you would have hated that, but it was
still in one piece a yard or so away. Cheek on the ground, I turned my
head enough to make out the stars above me, looking down. Then I felt
it again, this time in my neck, and that's when I knew what was happening. I was thinking of you inside the barn shivering as it all ran out
of me, but then I saw you a few minutes later stealing out past a spinney
of cottonwoods.

Afterwards, the police arrived and looked down at what a mess I was, nudging my sides with their boots. "He ain't the first bum to've come round here. They arrive with the seasons, like cottonwoods in bloom." Do you remember him saying that? I guess you wouldn't have heard, would you, gone by then. I like to think you did, though, because I know you would have been tickled and snorted in that horse manner of yours. Do you remember? Do you remember anything, Colton? A bar where we had our stomachs punched out. A car that broke down before we could even escape Kansas. A barn where cold wind passed from my skin to yours. The memory your trembling mouth betrayed to me of your son Scott, who'd taken his own life years before, nowhere near Vietnam. A dark sky thinned, like our jackets, by small holes of bright stars—that saw everything we did.

Do you?

Acknowledgments

Many thanks are owed and these but a few: my parents and step-parents, there are no words; my brothers: Brint, Bryan, Andy, and Mark; Papa and Big Dog, who are still alive in these pages; ZZ and Baby Stef; the Milward diaspora; the Segebrechts; Todd "the Clinic" Heitshusen; Ryan Lee Crosby; Chief, Nutso, Big D, all the ballers; KG and Shappi; Natey and Mighty T; the McThompsons, Tiger and Caruthers; Kate Sachaninson; Craig Eley, son of Robert Eley; Stuart Nadler; Christie Hodgen; Katie Chase; Skip Horack; John Jeremiah Sullivan; Charles Sumner and Monika Gehlawat; Michael Robbins; Judith Hoffman; Annika Blau; Jennifer Cannady; Cathy Bishop; the 2008 NCAA Basketball Champion Kansas Jayhawks; Amy Williams; the editors and staff of the magazines in which these stories first appeared; every student I've had the privilege to teach, as well as my own teachers: Marilynne Robinson, Ethan Canin, Lan Samantha Chang, James Alan McPherson, Naeem Murr, Marly Swick, Trudy Lewis, Aurelie Sheehan, and especially Ed Hagan, who was willing to read my first stories and still summon the grace to offer encouragement. I would also like to thank the people and institutions without whom this book would not exist: Jesse Lee Kercheval and the McCreight family of the University of Wisconsin's Institute for Creative Writing; Paul Douglass and Martha Heasley Cox of the Center for Steinbeck Studies at San Jose State University; the Virginia Center for the Creative Arts; the Santa Fe Art Institute; the Norman Mailer Colony; the Lannan Foundation; Connie Brothers and the Iowa Writers' Workshop; Bruce Wilcox and the staff at the University of Massachusetts Press; Steve Barthelme and the University of Southern Mississippi's Center for Writers. And lastly, huge thanks to Harriet Clark, dear friend, who is wicked smart and loves completely.

These stories first appeared in the following publications: "Quail Haven, 1989" in *Columbia*, no. 46 (Summer 2008); "Skywriting" in *The Southern*

Acknowledgments

Review 44, no. 4 (Autumn 2008); "The Agriculture Hall of Fame" in *Crazyhorse*, no. 67 (Spring 2005); "John" in *Avery*, no. 6 (Fall 2010). "Two Back, 1973" in *Fugue*, no. 33 (Fall 2007); "Birthday" in *Arts & Letters*, no. 18 (Fall 2007); "Ulysses" in *Confrontation*, no. 98/99 (Summer 2007); "The Cure for Cancer" in *The Literary Review* 48, no. 4 (Summer 2005); "The Antichrist Chronicles" in *Web Conjunctions* (as "Disappear") in December 2008, as well as in *Keeping the Wolves at Bay: Stories by Emerging American Writers*, edited by Sharon Dilworth (Autumn House Press, 2010); "Silver Creek, 1969" in *Failbetter*, no. 23 (Spring 2007).

The
Juniper
Prize

This volume is the seventh recipient of the Juniper Prize for Fiction, established in 2004 by the University of Massachusetts Press in collaboration with the UMass Amherst MFA Program for Poets and Writers, to be presented annually for an outstanding work of literary fiction. Like its sister award, the Juniper Prize for Poetry established in 1976, the prize is named in honor of Robert Francis (1901–1987), who lived for many years at Fort Juniper, Amherst, Massachusetts.